DOCTOR · WHO

STORYBOOK 2009

PANINI BOOKS

Contents

INTRODUCTION
A LETTER FROM THE DOCTOR.................5
Forwarded to us by Steven Moffat.

TEXT STORIES
HELLO CHILDREN, EVERYWHERE.........6
Written by Paul Magrs. Illustrations by Brian Williamson.

GRAND THEFT PLANET!...........................16
Written by James Moran. Illustrations by Daryl Joyce.

COLD...25
Written by Mark Gatiss. Illustrations by Ben Willsher.

BING BONG..42
Written by Gareth Roberts & Clayton Hickman.
Illustrations by Daniel McDaid.

ISLAND OF THE SIRENS.......................50
Written by Keith Temple. Illustrations by Adrian Salmon.

HOLD YOUR HORSES..........................60
Written by Nicholas Pegg. Illustrations by Jon Haward.

THE PUPLET......................................69
Written by Gary Russell. Illustrations by Andy Walker.

COMIC STRIP
THE IMMORTAL EMPEROR.....................34
Written by Jonathan Morris. Artwork by Rob Davis.

EDITOR & DESIGNER **CLAYTON HICKMAN**

FRONT COVER PAINTING BY **ALISTER PEARSON**

FRONTISPIECE PENCILS & INKS BY **DAVID A ROACH**   FRONTISPIECE COLOURS BY **JAMES OFFREDI**   CONTENTS PAGE ILLUSTRATION BY **BEN WILLSHER**

WITH THANKS TO **RUSSELL T DAVIES, DAVID TENNANT & CATHERINE TATE, GARY RUSSELL, EDWARD RUSSELL, PERI GODBOLD, TOM SPILSBURY, SCOTT GRAY, STUART MANNING, PETER WARE, RICHARD ATKINSON, DAVID TURBITT & BBC WORLDWIDE**

A Letter from the Doctor

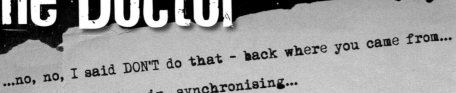

...no, no, I said DON'T do that - back where you came from...

...hang on, tuning in, synchronising...

...here we go, yes, yes...

...is this thing working? Can anyone read this?

Oh! There you all are! Hello readers, it's me, the Doctor. Don't look up, keep your eyes on the words, this is going to be a teensy, tiny bit tricky. No, seriously, keep reading, nice even pace, one word at a time. And stop frowning. Yeah, I can see you. All of you, actually - everyone who's reading these words, right now. Cluster telepath link, you see - Facebook, watch and weep!

Okay, better explain. I've been so late getting started on this introduction, I am now writing it LIVE. Yep, you read that right - this page is LIVE. These words are being written AS YOU READ THEM using temporal refraction isometry, and a typewriter. So please resist the temptation to skip ahead, cos I haven't written those bits yet. No, no, DON'T skip ahead, I said! Stop it - cos if you skip ahead and read, for instance, the very last word in this paragraph.................... oh, no, you all went and read it. And I panicked and stuck in any old word so you'd have something to read. FRUMBLE! In capitals. What does that even mean? That's not a word. And, look, now I have to work out a way to end this paragraph with the word FRUMBLE.

Seriously, the causal nexus can't take this kind of mucking about in it - so whatever you do, DON'T skip back to the first line of this introduction..........

..........or we'll end up trapped in causal loop. The entire readership of this Storybook, trapped forever in a causal loop on the first page - I'd never be asked for an introduction again!

Which would be a shame, cos this book is a belter. No really, it is, it's a belter of a Storybook, with that special ingredient - lots of ME. Hands on my hearts, I've read them all, and I honestly LOVED them - especially the two that haven't happened to me yet cos they're gonna come in really handy. And actually, I'm still in the middle of the last one, writing this introduction - see if you can spot where I find the time.

So off you go, enjoy. And please remember this page is live. That means, if you read it again, I have to write it again. And I'm a bit busy at the moment, so straight on to the stories, no popping back to the top of the page...

Happy times and places,   *The Doctor*

FORWARDED TO US BY **STEVEN MOFFAT**

Hello Children

WRITTEN BY **PAUL MAGRS**   ILLUSTRATIONS BY **BRIAN WILLIAMSON**

'I LOVED HER BOOKS WHEN I WAS A KID – BUT I DON'T SEE how they could have made a theme park out of them!' Donna did a slow twirl as she gazed about at The World of Aunty Winnie. It was 2025 and a portion of South London had been cleared aside to house this extraordinary, dreamlike place.

Only last night, in a diner orbiting Vantax 6, the subject of favourite childhood reading cropped up. The Doctor admitted to a long-running passion for the works of Beatrix Potter, which were required reading once upon a time at the Time Lord Academy. Donna laughed and explained that, as a little girl, she had read every book she could lay her hands upon, written by the mysterious and famous Aunty Winnie.

So the next thing was, the Doctor had found this place! This incredible theme park a little way into Donna's future, and now she was agog at the gingerbread houses, the oversized daffodils and daisies and the red-skinned pixies hopping about in the crowds of delighted visitors.

'It's… amazing!' Donna gasped, hugging the Doctor tight.

A small blue train filled with well-behaved children chugged by. A roller-coaster thundered overhead and did a careful loop-the-loop, its occupants giving out a very civilised, 'Hurrah!' Everything seemed tidy, safe, and very well organised. Not a blade of grass was out of place.

'Oh my god!' Donna grinned. 'I wonder if they've got Mr Tinkle!'

The Doctor started to laugh. 'Mr Who?'

Everywhere

She elbowed him. 'Shaddap. He was great. Like a little gnome, only he was really funny, right, and he used to drive around in his green car…'

Chuckling, the Doctor shook his head, following Donna through the complacently smiling throng. The Aunty Winnie factor seemed to bring out the best in visitors, he mused. People were queueing nicely, for instance. No one was grumbling. It was as if all the adults were being transported back to some simpler time in their youth. Some of the children, however, were looking bored.

A fluting female voice came over the loudspeakers: 'Hello children, everywhere! This is your Aunty Winnie! Welcome to my wonderful world of magic and fun and lots to do!'

Donna's eyes widened. 'It's really her! It's her voice! Aunty Winnie!'

'Nah, can't be, Donna. She'd be about... ooh, 160 years old by now.'

'Oh. Yeah.' Donna looked downcast.

It was while they were queueing up to go on the train that they witnessed the bust-up in the line ahead. A very tall rabbit was taking tickets, and he had caught a father sneaking an extra child aboard without paying. There was an eerie silence, then: 'You have done a bad thing!' cried the rabbit.

At first the man tried to laugh it off. He felt embarrassed being scolded in public. 'I won't be harassed by a giant bunny!' His wife pulled at his arm. 'Just pay him, Arthur.'

The Doctor and Donna could see that the rabbit was very cross indeed. Then, suddenly, he punched the man straight in the mouth, sending him crashing backwards into the immaculate shrubbery. 'You did a bad thing! You tried to steal!' The rabbit went bouncing after the man. 'Bad man! Bad man!'

The crowd drew back, appalled, as the bunny started stomping on the man with his overlarge feet.

'Stop!' The Doctor raced forward. 'Leave him alone!'

The bunny glared at him. 'He deserved punishment! And you will be next! No one misbehaves in the World of Aunty Winnie!'

The rabbit advanced, menacingly...

AT THE VERY HEART OF AUNTY WINNIE'S WORLD THERE stood a fairytale palace which was actually nothing of the sort. Inside it contained all of the complicated equipment that kept the theme park running smoothly and harmoniously.

That is to say, usually it was harmonious. But not today.

The manager was a short, elderly, nervous-looking man called Roger. That morning he was watching the screens in his office, supervising the eleven o'clock unicorn parade and the simultaneous penguin parascending display. An elf came to alert him to the fracas caused by the bunny running amok and stomping the visitor into the flower beds.

Roger covered his face with both hands. 'Why does it all go wrong for me?' he moaned. 'All I've tried to do is bring a little light and happiness into our visitors' drab lives.'

Last week it had been the flamingos. Someone's granny had been throwing rather nasty homemade buns from the shore of Flamingo Lake. In front of her grandchildren the flamingos had seized the old dear and dunked her, pelting her sodden form with inedible cakes. And now this.

Disasters like these could get a theme park shut down. And that couldn't be allowed to happen! They couldn't close the World of Aunty Winnie! Roger would *die*!

'Luckily, the bunny's victim was rescued by a couple of bystanders,' the elf told him. His tiny elfin fingers flickered over the controls till the screens displayed the Doctor interposing his lanky body and his spiky quiff between the irate rabbit and the pulverised father. 'He had some kind of sonic device that rendered the bunny immobile.'

Roger frowned. 'Did he, indeed?'

On the screens, the Doctor waved his sonic about, sending the bunny into conniptions, with blue sparks shooting out of his long, fluffy ears. Then he crashed backwards on the grass. 'Hurrah!' cried the frightened onlookers, politely.

Roger was transfixed by the image of the Doctor and Donna as they knelt to examine the prone rabbit. 'Who are these people, who can fettle our bunnies when they run wild?' he mused. Then he commanded the elf, 'Bring them to me! At once!'

DONNA, MEANWHILE, WAS CHOKING ON THE REEK OF smouldering blue fur. 'Is it some kind of robot? A rabbit robot?!'

The Doctor shook his head. 'Nah. Good guess, though. Look here, where its ears have burst open. You can see inside its workings...'

'Eurgh!' Donna pulled a face. 'What is that stuff?'

The Doctor produced an empty matchbox and scooped a blue, jelly-like substance out of the interior of the rabbit. The stuff quivered, almost alive, and the Doctor had to struggle to get a sample into the matchbox. Donna looked at him. 'The bunnies are filled with jelly?'

'What else?' he grinned, quirking his eyebrows in that maddening way of his.

Donna straightened up and tapped his shoulder. 'Party of elves on their way, Doctor,' she warned him. 'They're smiling all over their faces. But somehow, I don't think they're exactly happy.'

BY THE TIME ROGER MET THE DOCTOR AND DONNA HE was more his usual self, greeting them effusively in the main entrance of the palace. He conducted them on a short tour, all the while waxing enthusiastically about the Wonderful World of Aunty Winnie.

'It's all my idea, Doctor. All my concept. It's the dream of my childhood come true.'

'Right, I see,' nodded the Doctor, looking interested.

'Like many millions of children worldwide I was mesmerized by the tales spun by my magical Aunty. I wanted them to go on forever. I wanted to live inside them…'

'Donna was saying just the same thing to me earlier,' said the Doctor. Donna gave a sickly smile. She didn't like this shrewd and sweaty old man knowing anything about her. She didn't trust the way his comb-over was so precisely, suspiciously tidy.

'When poor Aunty Winnie passed away…' he was saying.

'Aunty Winnie died!' gasped the Doctor, giving Donna a sidelong look. She scowled at him.

'Oh, years ago!' said Roger, waving a pudgy hand. 'She'd be 160 if she were alive today! Anyway, we envisaged this place as a kind of living memorial to her.'

The Doctor stared around approvingly. 'And a very impressive job you've made of it. With all the very lifelike elves and, um… things.' A couple of gossamer-winged fairies had fluttered in to serve them tea and biscuits. 'Thank you,' Donna told them, feeling disconcerted, and wondering whether these creatures were filled with glistening jelly as well.

Roger was still going on: 'I see this place as my chance to roll time back to a golden period in my own life. A more innocent time. A time when I felt safe in the world my Aunty Winnie described. A world of decency and goodness…'

'Yeah, bit simplistic though, isn't it?' said Donna, through a mouthful of cake. 'I mean, I loved her books as a kid, but you can't really use them as a philosophy for the rest of your life. "The world according to Winnie" or whatever.'

Roger was looking at her strangely. 'Don't you think so, miss? I believe that people want the world to be simpler. Children today aren't really very happy at all, with their techno gizmos and their complicated whatsits.'

The Doctor raised an eyebrow. 'And yet, Roger me old mate, this place itself is higher than high-tech.'

'True,' sighed Roger. 'Only in order to give an illusion of happy, innocent, fairytale simplicity on the surface.'

'It's all a bit too much on the surface for me,' Donna muttered. 'And what about these malfunctions, eh? What about that poor bloke in the queue?'

'The elves whizzed him away to the Happy Trails emergency room. He's fine.' Then Roger's face darkened. 'But it's true. Things have been going awry in Winnie's World recently.'

Just at that moment, as if on cue, bright lights started pulsating and a terrible klaxon wailed. The Doctor bolted from his chair and led the others at a run to see what was going wrong now. It was all too evident on the myriad screens.

Donna's mouth dropped open in shock. 'Mr Tinkle!'

The Doctor stared at her. 'What?'

'It's Mr Tinkle! My all-time favourite Aunty Winnie character!'

In his little green car, a life-sized Mr Tinkle – the funny little elf – was going on a mad rampage. He was sending the crowds scattering as he accelerated his motor and prepared to ram-raid his way through the park's main entrance.

'Mr Tinkle has gone beserk!' Roger screamed into the controls, plunging the whole complex into Red Alert.

MR TINKLE HAD HAD ENOUGH. THE WORLD OF AUNTY Winnie was much too small for him. And so – smash, crash, tinkle! – he drove his little green car up to the main gates and bashed his way to freedom. Children screamed, mothers fled, pixies scrambled to report his errant behaviour to their superiors. Mr Tinkle had turned bad!

He gritted his teeth and revved his engine and the bells on his hat jingle-jangled as he thundered his way onto the main street and the real world beyond. Here, Saturday shoppers and unwary pedestrians were horrified at the sight of the overgrown elf. He parped his horn at kids misbehaving. He bashed into double-parked cars. And, when he noticed an old man stepping into the traffic before looking both ways first – Mr Tinkle promptly tried to run him over. That would teach the naughty fellow a lesson!

THE DOCTOR, DONNA AND ROGER WERE FIGHTING TO STAY upright in the panicking tide of people fleeing this scene of disaster. 'How do we switch him off?' Donna demanded. 'Doctor, use your screwdriver again!'

The Doctor frowned. 'I can't get a fix on him. He's veering round all over the place!' It was true, they saw, as they clambered over the rubble Mr Tinkle had left in his wake. His little car was hurtling hectically up the high street and it was almost out of sight.

Roger had gone into shock. 'But none of them have ever escaped before,' he moaned. 'It isn't possible. None of them can leave Aunty Winnie's World…'

'Well, they have now,' said the Doctor grimly. 'You can't control these things, can you? You've really no idea how they work, do you?' He seized Roger by the shoulders. 'Do you?!'

There came a tremendous crashing and banging as, somewhere further up the street, Mr Tinkle started ramming his car into the barrows of street vendors selling illegal imitation handbags and watches. Roger cringed. 'I *do* know how to control them! They are my magical creatures! I am their friend! They do what I say!'

'Hello? Real world calling!' Donna was exasperated. 'Just look at the state of this place!'

The Doctor grabbed the squirming man by his suit lapels. 'Why are your magical friends going bananas, Rog? That's what we need to know!'

'I… don't know!' wailed Roger.

'Is it to do with all the blue jelly stuff inside of them?' Donna yelled. 'Is that what it is?'

'Blue jelly?' cried Roger. 'Blue jelly?'

The Doctor looked disgusted. 'Donna, take him back to his fake palace. Calm him down and see if you can't get any more sense out of him. See if those fairies have got a drop of brandy knocking about the place.'

She looked doubtful. 'What about you?'

He straightened up and faced the street. 'I'm gonna go and deal with Mr Tinkle.'

As Donna led the quivering manager of the deadly theme park back to safety she was thinking about how far-removed all this was from the World of Aunty Winnie she had carried about in her head all these years. This was like a sick, horrible version of Winnie's world. And it was all because of this pathetic man walking with her. She just *knew* it was his fault.

The tannoy burst into life, filling the disturbed air of the park with the dulcet tones of Aunty Winnie herself: 'Oh, dear, children! It seems that Mr Tinkle has had a funny turn! Never mind! He'll soon be out of his naughty mood. But he deserves a good slap, doesn't he? He deserves a punch up the hooter! All bad little people should get a slap when they're being meddlesome and naughty!'

Donna was glad when the creepy voice cut out. She hastened Roger towards his palace in the park's centre. She became aware of a new noise, a distant patter of – what was it? – flapping and cracking. 'What the hell's that?'

'Oh, my God,' Roger said. 'It's the pixies. They've started slapping people…'

'YOU MUST AGREE MY AUNTY WINNIE WAS A WONDERFUL woman,' Roger was saying, as he led Donna back into the palace. Inside, alarms were going off, as elfin workers went scurrying in various states of panic. They even came upon a fretful teddy bear, who didn't seem to know what to do with himself.

Donna snapped, 'We could do with less chat and a bit more action, actually, sunshine. The Doctor's out there, doing battle with Mr Tinkle!' She paused and shook her head. 'I can't believe I'm even saying that! You've gotta find a way of helping him! Switch 'em all off, or something!'

Roger looked shocked. 'Switch them all off? All my magical friends? Then who would I have? Why, I'd be all alone!'

'Are you honestly telling me that the creatures in here are your only friends in the world?'

'Of course! Since Aunty died, I've had no one… no one to look after me.' The little man looked as if he might cry, and suddenly Donna felt sorry for shouting at him.

She hustled him into his main control room, where the array of view screens gave them a better sense of what was going on. What they learned wasn't at all reassuring. It seemed that many of the teddy bears, fairies and prancing ponies had gone completely bonkers that afternoon.

'But they're such happy, docile creatures!' Roger wailed. He turned savagely to Donna. 'It's you! You and your loopy, skinny friend! Things only started going wrong when you two turned up. You've gone and jinxed Winnie's World!'

Donna was about to warn him he'd better shut his mouth, when the loudspeakers crackled again and the disembodied tones of Aunty Winnie called out, 'Punish them, my dears! Punish all the naughty people! All the queue jumpers! The litter louts! The walkers-on-the-grass! Slap them, pixies! Trample on them, my pretty ponies!'

'This place is mental!' Donna cried, staring in disbelief at the multi-coloured carnage being unleashed on the screens.

'Oh, if only Aunty Winnie really were here,' Roger sobbed. 'She'd know what to do. She brought me up, you know. When my own parents were killed in a freak fairground accident. She took me in and looked after me and made me feel safe…'

Donna stared at him. 'She was your actual real-life Aunty?!'

He nodded. 'Of course. I am her only nephew and heir. I am the only one left to protect her legacy. But look what's happening! Chaos! Murder! Why is it all going wrong? Why has everything gone haywire?'

Before Donna could hazard a guess, there was a great crash and two fairies and a giant teddy bear arrived in Roger's control room. They fluttered and lumbered menacingly towards the two humans. Their eyes were dead and their faces were frozen into rictus grins.

'Oh my God,' said Donna. 'They're here to get us, aren't they?'

'Go back to your work!' Roger shrieked. 'You're meant to be selling ice cream, you three! What are you doing here? Get away from us!'

'Bad Roger,' said the Teddy, in a gruff voice.

'Bad Donna,' shrilled the fairies in unison. 'Donna's been a very bad girl…'

Donna wasn't sticking around to hear any more of this creepy weirdness. She grabbed Roger by the scruff of his sweaty neck. 'Run!'

◆ ◆ ◆

MEANWHILE THE DOCTOR HAD PAUSED IN HIS ATTEMPT TO curb the destruction unleashed on the street outside by Mr Tinkle and his little green car. Innocent bystanders had been scattered and strewn across pavements, and the plate glass fronts of shops had been smashed to smithereens – all accompanied by the cheery tinkling of the bells in Mr T's hat and his eerie little chuckle.

However close the Doctor could get to him, it wasn't close enough to put the deadly elf out of action. Instead, the Doctor pelted back to the TARDIS, which was parked near the entrance to Winnie's World. He noticed that the police had arrived and were looking very unsure about the gigantic kitten that was guarding the only way into the park.

The Doctor managed to slip unnoticed into his police box and, once inside, started work on examining the queer splodge of jelly he'd stuffed into his matchbox. At first the instrument panels shivered in disgust and would have nothing to do with the strangely chilly substance. But the Doctor needed to know what it was. Was it inside all of the creatures? He prodded at the blue lump. It seemed to seethe and hiss at him angrily. And then the TARDIS instruments grudgingly gave him some answers: yes, the matter was not from Earth. This little scrap on the console was but one millionth of the whole creature. It was screaming in outrage because the Doctor had ripped it away from the rest of itself…

'Some kind of gestalt entity,' the Doctor murmured. 'Or just one huge great jelly in different moulds. Jelly shaped and flavoured… who by, though, hmmm?' He gave the jelly an experimental lick. Horrible taste. The thing seized his tongue for a split second and the Doctor almost panicked. He ripped the creature away from him. 'Whoah, jelly!'

Then he glanced at the scanner screen, to see Mr Tinkle still causing mayhem in the entrance to a shopping mall, where surprised squeals were rapidly turning to howls of terror. The Doctor decided that the time had come for him to intervene decisively.

He glared at the blob of jelly. He knew that it wanted to be reunited with the rest of its vile self. Surely what animated Mr Tinkle was the same rotten stuff. Perhaps he could let the jelly do his work for him… and draw Mr Tinkle to where the Doctor wanted him.

Then the Doctor blurred into action, tapping and rapping at the complicated instrument panels of the TARDIS. He took the ship on a short hop, landing directly in front of Mr Tinkle's madly-revving vehicle. He dashed madly around the console, winding a loop of twine around various switches and levers, sparks flying from the complaining controls. He'd rigged up a small but super-powerful force field, which he could activate at a moment's notice using his sonic. Hopefully.

Then, throwing all the switches and dials he could reach at once, the Doctor ran to the doors and flung them open – leaving the way into the TARDIS clear.

Mr Tinkle tinkled his bells. His engine roared like a crazed bull. He felt the glob of jelly calling out to him from within the alien vehicle. '*Free me!*' the jelly called out to Mr Tinkle. '*Come and save me from this awful man!*'

To the further astonishment of the bystanders in the mall, Mr Tinkle drove his green car straight at the TARDIS… which promptly swallowed him up.

The wooden doors slammed shut.

INSIDE, THE DOCTOR WHIPPED THE FORCE FIELD INTO action, and it gave a glorious shimmer of gold. He wielded it like a matador does his cape. It worked! Mr Tinkle's car slewed to a dead halt. Both it and Mr Tinkle and the glob of blue jelly were caught fast by the force field. Trapped by the Doctor!

'Gotcha!' the Doctor cried in triumph.

Mr Tinkle glared at him and said something very naughty indeed.

Just as the Doctor stepped forward, something weird started to happen. Mr Tinkle and his car were melting. They were liquefying and glistening and dripping into an enormous splodge of blue jelly on the TARDIS floor…

'I THOUGHT THEY WERE GONNA KILL US,' DONNA panted, as the great doors clanged behind them. The fairies and the galumphing teddy had caught them easily, shoving their human prisoners into these dank and grimy catacombs beneath the palace. Donna sniffed. There was a strange, hospitally smell down here.

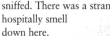

'Kill us?' Roger laughed, wildly. 'Why, they would hardly kill me, would they?'

'Why not?' Donna snapped. 'Because you're their king? King of the magical beasties? I never saw them taking much notice of you when you were screaming at them to put you down!'

Roger looked shamefaced. His cheeks glowed hotly in the clammy gloom. 'It's true. The whole place has gone wrong. And I don't know why.'

'Where does that blue jelly stuff come from, Roger?' Donna demanded. 'I think it's time you spilled the beans.'

He hid his face in his hands. 'I never meant any harm. It seemed like such miraculous stuff. So harmless…'

Donna stared at him levelly. 'Go on. Tell me.'

'I was just a boy.' Roger lowered his voice, as if he thought the creatures above ground might be listening in. 'It was shortly after I was orphaned and moved in with my Aunty Winnie. She wasn't yet a world-famous authoress. She wasn't yet the Aunty Winnie we all know and love.'

Donna pulled a face. She was beginning to wish she had never heard of Aunty Winnie. As Roger talked he was leading the two of them through the dingy tunnels. Even with this tiny amount of light, Donna realised, he could still find his way about. As if he knew exactly where he was going…

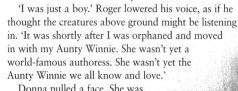

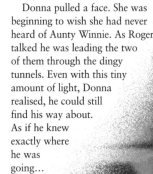

'The day the jelly came, I remember all too well.' Donna realised Roger was shaking in his shoes. 'Aunty Winnie's publisher threw a big party for the publication of the first Mr Tinkle book. All the press were there. It was a garden party in the grounds of Aunty Winnie's beloved Daffodil Villas. Hordes of local children were in attendance. And I hated them. Already I was used to being the only special child at Daffodil Villas.'

Donna stared at him. He sounded like a terrible kid! But then, she'd been no angel herself at that age.

'Anyway,' Roger went on, 'as they were bringing round the jelly and ice cream I realised that my helping of jelly was... *different* to everyone else's. It spoke to me!'

Donna almost laughed. 'Are you sure?'

'The jelly had sought me out especially!'

Donna shook her head. Crazy.

Roger went on. 'It was Borace Gamnetyaac, an entity from the Magenta Spool galaxy, fallen accidentally through a rent in time and space, and dropped there, in the gardens of Daffodil Villas, at the mercy of the human race.'

The tunnels were narrowing and the air growing staler. Donna seriously wondered where the little man was leading her. 'But what did this Bora... Borrga... jelly stuff want with you? You were just a little boy.'

Roger looked sly. 'The Gamnetyaac entity thrives off imaginative stimulation. It feeds on ideas and dreams. Even as it gorges, it amplifies the mental energies and... it can make them real! I introduced Borace Gamnetyaac to my Aunty Winnie's marvellous imagination!'

'But... why?' Donna asked. 'Why would you lead an alien to your Aunty?'

'Because Borace could infuse her stories with real magic. Borace Gamnetyaac could bring her money, success, fame, immortality. And the Gamnetyaac entity could bring her characters literally to life. Isn't that what Aunty Winnie wanted?'

Donna frowned. 'Did you ever ask her?'

Roger chuckled. 'I knew my Aunty well. And by introducing her to Borace I made her the most famous children's author in the world!'

Then Donna realised they were standing in front of a shiny wooden door.

'Ah,' said Roger. 'We're here.'

● ◉ ●

THE DOCTOR RACED LIKE A MADMAN THROUGH THE WRECKAGE of the World of Aunty Winnie. Somehow, in the few minutes he'd been busy aboard the TARDIS, creating a trap for Mr Tinkle and getting him to revert to blue jelly, the theme park had gone into full-scale self-destruct mode.

He found a purple pony lying by the ice cream stand. Its leg had been broken in all the confusion, and it was leaking blue jelly. 'Don't show me compassion,' it snarled, which rather startled the Doctor. 'You who has part of the Borace Gamnetyaac entity under lock and key! You're making things worse!' The pony glared at the Doctor, and snorted.

'I'm trying to help,' said the Doctor gently. 'This destruction needs to stop. Right now. It might have started as a laugh for you creatures, but...'

'A laugh?' squealed the pony – and coughed up blue jelly. His whole body was wracked with pain, the Doctor realised: he had been badly hurt in the stampede for the exits. 'We aren't doing this for fun. Are you mad?'

The Doctor looked confused. 'Then why? Why are you doing it?'

The pony sighed. His life force seemed to be leaving him. 'All we have tried to do is create a happy place on Earth. A magical place. A place just like our own home in the Magenta Spool. With Roger's help we thought we might achieve that. We thought we could make ourselves and some of the humans happy...'

'What happened, then?' asked the Doctor urgently. 'Why did you spoil it?' He gestured at the ruinous, smouldering theme park around them. A giant teddy lumbered past, looking for fresh human victims, and the Doctor had to duck down behind a candy-striped litter bin.

'We didn't spoil it, Doctor,' coughed the pony. '*She* did.'

The Doctor boggled. 'Who?'

The pony lowered his tired head in defeat as the loudspeakers above them blared out: 'Will the Doctor

please stop harassing
dying pretty ponies and report
forthwith to the underground inner sanctum
of his darling Aunty Winnie?'

'You're not my darling aunty,' the Doctor muttered rebelliously.

'Oh yes I am, you silly man!' the loudspeakers cried triumphantly.

At that moment, a blubbering, slobbering sound reached the Doctor's ears. Whirling around he saw an enormous, quivering lump of the blue jelly wobbling up the path towards him. With a squelch, the pony suddenly dissolved into the same slimy substance, and then launched itself at the bigger creature and was absorbed into it.

The Doctor raised his hands. 'Take me to your Aunty,' he sighed.

⬡ ⬡ ⬡

DONNA DIDN'T KNOW WHAT SHE WAS GOING TO SEE AS
Roger led her into the inner sanctum. During her time with the Doctor she had already seen some pretty hair-raising things, but nothing could have prepared her for what Aunty Winnie looked like nowadays.

'Welcome, Donna Noble!' The voice was accompanied by a strange tap-tap-tapping noise. It went on, 'You were once in my fan club, weren't you? We still have you in our records! You were a devoted fan of Aunty Winnie!'

Donna stepped hesitantly into the sepulchral room, trying to make out the figure lying on the chaise longue. It was beckoning to her, calling out in a crackling, electronic voice, that weird tapping accompanying every word.

'Oh my God! Aunty Winnie? You're still alive?'

'I'm 160 years young, dear! And I'm still in control of all my faculties! Didn't you guess, my child? I've been in command from the start. Isn't that correct, Roger?'

'Oh yes, Aunty Winnie,' simpered Roger, nudging Donna forward with his elbow. 'Go to her, Donna. Let Aunty see you.'

Donna realised that this room was the source of the hospitally smell. There was an array of life support machines keeping the old woman ticking. Donna gave a short gasp. Old woman? There was precious little old woman left. Now she was close to the chaise longue, Donna could see that all that remained of Aunty Winnie was a baleful eye in a jar, one withered hand, some brain cells in a saucer and a yellowing foot, all wired up together. Next to these horrid remains was an old-fashioned typewriter, at which the toes of the foot and the fingers

of the hand were tapping continuously. The words they spelled were transmitted instantly over the loudspeaker.

'I'm afraid I'm not looking my best, my dear,' Aunty Winnie typed out.

Donna felt unwell. 'W-why are you hiding away down here?'

Aunty Winnie laughed. 'Do my fans really want to see me like this? They want the world to be a happy, pretty place…' Donna thought she could detect a sardonic edge to the woman's words.

'But the world *isn't* always happy or pretty, is it?' Donna said pointedly. Didn't she just know it!

'Quite,' Aunty Winnie agreed, and her single jaundiced eye swivelled to stare nastily at Roger. 'It's not a happy, pretty place to live in when your life has been hideously prolonged like mine has! Especially against your will!'

Donna gasped. 'He's keeping you alive against your will?'

'Hush now,' Roger chuckled uneasily. 'We've been over this a thousand times, Aunty.'

'I've had enough!' Aunty Winnie wailed, her wrinkled hand and foot tapping like mad at the typewriter keys. 'I'm a tired out old woman! I don't want to live in Aunty Winnie's world anymore!'

Roger hung his head – but his voice was steely. 'I'm sorry about that, Aunty Winnie.'

Then there was a whirl of activity as the Doctor came hurrying in, brandishing his sonic screwdriver. The enormous blue jelly creature sat quivering in the doorway behind him.

'Whew!' he yelled, and Donna could have punched the air at the sight of him. 'That took some doing! Putting pixies and teddies and monkeys and fairies out of action, one after the next! I was starting to feel like the villain in a fairytale!' He grinned at Donna. 'And I'm so much better suited to rescuing princesses, shining armour, that sort of thing.'

'Do they do armour in extra skinny?' Donna smirked back at her friend.

The Doctor ignored the jibe. 'That blue jelly stuff is a nightmare to deal with. It's from the Magenta Spool galaxy you know, Donna. And it's called Borace Gamnetyaac and it's keen to go home, and I'm keen to help it. Oh! Hello, Roger. And – who's this? Aunty Winnie, I presume?'

The ancient toes typed and Winnie said, 'Greetings, Doctor. You have arrived just in time for the end.'

'Oh dear,' frowned the Doctor. 'Not much of Aunty Winnie left, is there? I'm so sorry. How cruel.' He boggled his eyes furiously at Roger.

'Doctor,' said Aunty Winnie. 'Can you really send the Gamnetyaac home?'

'Yep,' he grinned. 'Course!'

'And can you free me? Can you let me rest?'

He looked grave. 'If that's what you want.'

'Nooo!' shrieked Roger. 'You can't take my Aunty Winnie away! She's all I've got!' Roger fought his way past Donna to the Doctor.

'Watch it, Roger!' Donna warned. 'Haven't you done enough?'

'Me?' he asked, quite stung.

'All that mess outside. Those poor injured people. That was all down to you, wasn't it?' Donna accused.

The Doctor smiled, grimly. 'Oh no. It was all down to Aunty Winnie here, wasn't it... dear?' He looked sadly at the remains of the brilliant old woman. Her foot and hand and eye looked quite shifty. 'You were intent on destroying the World of Aunty Winnie, weren't you?'

The fingers typed almost reluctantly. 'Oh, you are an old clever clogs, Doctor,' she said. 'I was so desperate to draw attention to my plight! All I had to do was turn my magical land into a bad place...'

All hope had drained out of Roger. 'It worked, your plan, Aunty. It's finished. All of it.'

But, as it turned out, the Doctor had other ideas. 'Aha!' he beamed at them all. 'Not when you've got someone here who's an expert on happy endings!'

'YOU SEE,' THE DOCTOR SMILED, AS ROGER HELPED HIM wheel Aunty Winnie's remains aboard the TARDIS, the blue jelly blubbering in behind them, 'the Magenta Spool is remarkably like the world your Aunty envisaged in her books. Unicorns, bunnies, the lot!'

Aunty Winnie typed excitedly in transit. 'The world in my head is real?'

'How could it not be? With Borace helping you imagine for all these years?' The Doctor hurried to set the coordinates. 'We're going there now.'

'I- I don't know how to thank you,' Roger said.

'It's your Aunty I'm doing it for,' said the Doctor. 'Maybe it's payback for all her work. Five hundred books, wasn't it, Donna? She deserves a reward, I think. Well, now I'm giving Borace Gamnetyaac a better idea for what kind of form he should adopt...'

Borace seemed to understand the Doctor's idea at once, and to approve. They watched then as a small portion of the blue jelly shimmered, broke away from the rest, and crept over Aunty Winnie's remaining flesh and typewriter. A new shape was forming. Soon there was a sprightly old woman sitting there, sporting a blue-rinsed perm and a smart tweed suit. Roger cried out in shock.

'Almost there,' the Doctor grinned at the astonished Donna. 'And Aunty Winnie's just about ready to face a world just like the one inside her own head.'

Donna shook her own head in disbelief. She and the Doctor watched as Roger sat down on the chaise longue beside his newly-reborn Aunty. His legs were swinging and he held her hand as the TARDIS wheezed and groaned its way onto the grassy hills of the Magenta Spool. Roger looked like all his happy birthdays had come at once.

'Are you both sitting comfortably?' the Doctor asked, his eyes twinkling. He pressed a switch on the console and the police box doors slammed open, golden sunlight pouring into the craft. The larger part of Borace wobbled outside, joyously.

Aunty Winnie turned her head and stared at her new home. She squeezed her nephew's hand. 'Then we can begin. Again,' she said.

THE END

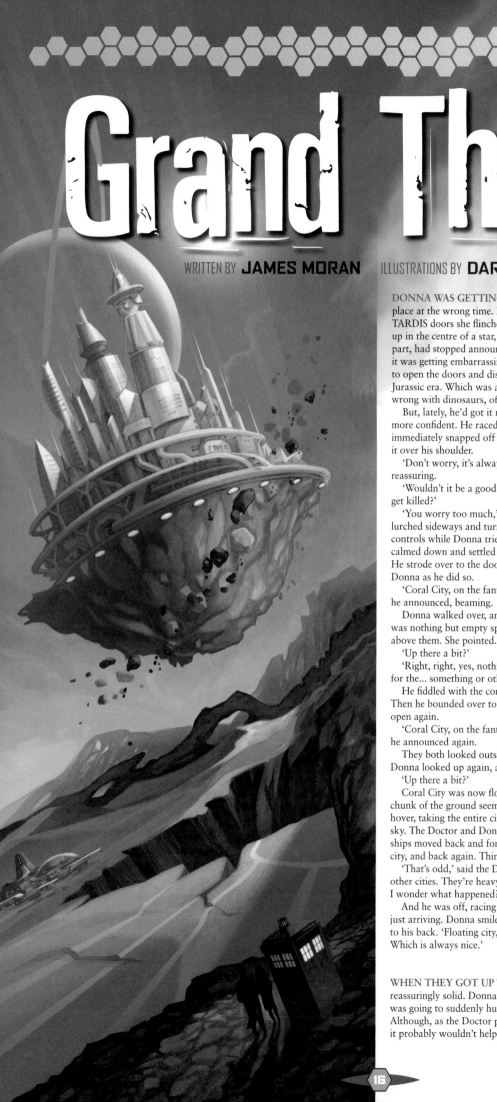

Grand Theft P

WRITTEN BY **JAMES MORAN**   ILLUSTRATIONS BY **DARYL JOYCE**

DONNA WAS GETTING USED TO ARRIVING IN THE WRONG place at the wrong time. Now, every time the Doctor flung open the TARDIS doors she flinched slightly, wondering if they were going to end up in the centre of a star, or in the middle of a battle. The Doctor, for his part, had stopped announcing where and when they had arrived because it was getting embarrassing. 'San Francisco,' he'd shout happily, only to open the doors and discover that they were in Dagenham. In the late Jurassic era. Which was a bit more ancient and, well, dinosaury. Nothing wrong with dinosaurs, of course. But they did tend to try to eat you.

But, lately, he'd got it right several times in a row and was feeling more confident. He raced around the console and pulled a lever – which immediately snapped off in his hand. Donna stared at it, but he just threw it over his shoulder.

'Don't worry, it's always doing that,' he said. Which wasn't exactly reassuring.

'Wouldn't it be a good idea to fix it, then?' asked Donna. 'So we don't get killed?'

'You worry too much,' replied the Doctor, just before the TARDIS lurched sideways and turned itself inside out. He wrestled with the controls while Donna tried to figure out which way was up. Things calmed down and settled again. The Doctor looked up and grinned. He strode over to the doors and flung them open, looking back at Donna as he did so.

'Coral City, on the fantastic leisure planet of Splendorosa!' he announced, beaming.

Donna walked over, and coughed. The Doctor turned around. Outside was nothing but empty space. Donna looked up, and saw a planet far above them. She pointed.

'Up there a bit?'

'Right, right, yes, nothing to worry about, probably didn't compensate for the... something or other. Hang on!'

He fiddled with the controls, and the central column rose and fell once. Then he bounded over to the doors, followed by Donna. He flung them open again.

'Coral City, on the fantastic leisure planet of Splendorosa!' he announced again.

They both looked outside at a massive canyon in the ground. Donna looked up again, and pointed.

'Up there a bit?'

Coral City was now floating several hundred feet up in the air. A large chunk of the ground seemed to have ripped itself out and gone for a hover, taking the entire city with it. It was stable, level, just... up in the sky. The Doctor and Donna stepped out to get a better look. Transport ships moved back and forth, ferrying passengers from the ground to the city, and back again. Things seemed to be running smoothly.

'That's odd,' said the Doctor. 'It used to be on the ground. Like most other cities. They're heavy like that, usually works out better that way. I wonder what happened? Come on!'

And he was off, racing towards one of the transport ships that was just arriving. Donna smiled and started to follow him. 'Sure,' she said, to his back. 'Floating city, why not? At least nobody's tried to kill us yet. Which is always nice.'

● ◆ ●

WHEN THEY GOT UP TO THE CITY, THE STREETS WERE reassuringly solid. Donna stamped around a bit to make sure that nothing was going to suddenly hurtle to the ground, hundreds of feet below. Although, as the Doctor pointed out, if it *was* going to fall, stamping on it probably wouldn't help. Looking around, they noticed lots of signs

lanet!

that had been hastily re-painted to add the words 'THE FABULOUS FLOATING' just before 'Coral City'.

'Hmm,' said the Doctor. 'Must have been fairly recent, then.'

'That or they're all skinflints,' replied Donna. 'My local pub still has "Mandy's Famous Pub Lunches" on the sign outside, but Mandy moved to Spain twenty years ago. And they don't do lunches any more. And it's a mobile phone shop now.'

'Why'd you leave that till last? I'd have thought that was the most pertinent piece of information.'

'In spaceman logic, maybe.'

'We need to find someone who'd know. Can't tell who are locals and who are tourists. Ah! That looks likely!'

The Doctor raced off towards a building marked 'Jellop's Tourist Information Centre'. As he did, he called back over his shoulder: 'Let's hope it's not a mobile phone shop!'

INSIDE, THEY WERE RELIEVED TO DISCOVER THAT IT WAS still a tourist information centre. What's more, Jellop was still there, and more than eager to give them the grand tour. Five minutes and two rows of dusty old ceremonial armour later, the grand tour was over, and Jellop sat them down in front of a rickety screen. He slapped the projector until it clattered into life, and waited proudly while it talked them through the story of Coral City.

According to the narrator, who sounded suspiciously like Jellop putting on a posh voice, the ground on Splendorosa contained high levels of strontilite, an unusually magnetic metal. The soil was flecked with it, and occasionally random fragments spontaneously changed their polarity. Ten years ago, all of the strontilite under Coral City suddenly changed polarity, and became repelled by the ground underneath and around it – which meant the foundations of the city ripped themselves out of the ground, and hovered up in the air. Like two opposing magnets that repel each other. Except really, really, *really* big. Many tests were done – demonstrated on the screen by a bad actor dressed up as a scientist, who looked suspiciously like Jellop in a fake beard and white coat – which concluded that a sudden polarity change was the cause, as everyone had expected. Massive stabilisers were built to keep the city steady, several ferries were put into operation, and the city became more popular than ever.

'Hang on a minute,' said the Doctor.

'The presentation's not actually quite finished yet,' said Jellop, hopping from one foot to another. He didn't get many visitors, and wanted everything to go smoothly.

'Yeah, but – what *made* it change polarity? Bit of a coincidence that so much of this strontilite stuff should change in the one place, don't you think? Well, you probably don't, you're not a scientist I suppose, speaking of which, who did these tests?'

Jellop looked through some sheets of paper, trying to remember. This wasn't in his tourist script, so he had to look it up. He found the relevant piece of paper, and held it up triumphantly.

'Geocorp!' he announced. 'Geocorp, they did the tests, and very thorough they were too, they checked, er, all of the ground, with their little, um, ground... checking machines.'

The Doctor beamed at him. 'So why don't I go and have a chat with them. Donna, you coming?'

Donna folded her arms. 'Hmm, go and see some scientist talk about geological surveys, or stay in the riveting tourist information centre? How *do* I choose?'

'If it helps,' said Jellop, 'we have a set of special massage chairs that you might like to try. A demonstration of the unique properties of the strontilite. Each chair contains lots of specially ground dust from –'

'There you go,' said the Doctor, already halfway out the door. 'Massage chairs, you check them out, won't be long.'

'Oh he's always doing that,' complained Donna. 'C'mon then, let's see these chairs, then.'

THE DOCTOR STRODE UP TO THE RECEPTION DESK AT Geocorp's enormous offices and flashed his psychic paper at the woman behind the desk as he passed by.

'Here to see the boss. I'm the Director of the Geological Society. Don't get up, I'll let myself in. This way, is it?'

'Sir, you can't just–'

But the Doctor walked straight into the main lift, grinning at the flustered receptionist.

'I know! Naughty, aren't I?'

The lift doors pinged open at the top floor. A pair of ornate double doors faced the Doctor across the corridor. He flung them open with a grin. Inside was a large, luxurious office, with a large, luxurious man seated behind a desk. The man, according to the brass nameplate on the desk, was Volsairius Trefgar, CEO. And his face was turning several interesting shades of purple.

'What is the meaning of this?' barked Trefgar. 'You can't just waltz in here, I'm the CEO!'

'Ah, yes, well, your receptionist said that too, but the thing is, I just did. I know I did, because I'm here. Didn't waltz though. More of a march. Anyway, hello! I'm the Doctor. Geological Society. Blimey that's a nice view.'

He flashed the psychic paper again as he wandered over to the huge picture window. It was indeed a nice view, of the whole city.

'How do people know what the view is going to be like?' continued the Doctor. 'I mean, when you start building something, you're on the ground, you don't know what the view'll be like from the fiftieth floor, do you? Can't exactly build the whole thing, then get to the top, and say ooh, can we shift it a bit to the left?'

Trefgar stood up. 'You're here on business, from the Geological Society?' he asked.

'That's right, great bunch they are too... *we* are, I mean.'

'Well? What is it?'

'Sorry, yeah, just a few questions about the whole hovering thing. Going over exactly how it happened.'

'Everyone knows how it happened. The ground of Splendorosa is flecked with an unusually magnetic–'

'Yeah, yeah, I know all the publicity blurb, I've been to the tourist centre. My mate's there now, checking out their massage chairs. Fascinating metal, that strontilite. Thing is, I just don't see how a massive patch of it could suddenly all change polarity at the same time. And I'm not seeing how it'd be strong enough to lift an entire city. I'm just not seeing it, Trefgar me old mucker.'

'Then perhaps you should look more closely at the survey.'

'That's right, the survey. Which Geocorp did. You wouldn't have all the raw data handy, would you? Just so we could, you know... double check all the figures and make sure nothing was missed?'

Trefgar stared at the Doctor, his eyes narrowing.

'I assure you, sir, that nothing was missed. We went over the data

several times ourselves. What other explanation could there be? Do you think the city simply became tired of being on the ground? Perhaps it floated up into the air of its own accord?'

The Doctor looked back at Trefgar, getting more serious now.

'In my experience, Trefgar, things are never quite as simple as they seem. But you won't mind letting me see that raw data, will you? Nothing to be concerned about, is there?'

'Of course not. But I cannot let anyone outside the company see the raw data. Our methods are highly confidential. I wouldn't want our competitors discovering exactly how we do things here.'

'And exactly how *do* you do things here, Trefgar?'

There was an awkward silence, until Trefgar smiled.

'As I said. Our methods are confidential. But as the analysis survey results are a matter of public record, I suggest you double check those back at the tourist office. Yes, our guest was just leaving.'

The last part was directed to the large, burly men who had suddenly appeared behind the Doctor to escort him out.

'Oh, hello. You're quite large, aren't you? Well, I'd better be off, taken up too much of your time already. It's all right, I'll see myself out.'

The Doctor left, followed by the two large men. The doors closed.

Trefgar reached for a button on his desk and called up a communications screen. Static fizzed then cleared to show an ugly, pug-faced alien. It didn't look happy at all.

'Did you hear all of that?' asked Trefgar.

'Yes! Get rid of him!' shouted the alien.

'I did. He's gone.'

'No! Get rid of him. Rid! *Rid!*'

'Oh. I see. As you wish.'

The alien harrumphed, and the screen went blank. Trefgar shook his head with distaste. 'Terrible conversationalists.'

He took a small computer control device out of his desk drawer, and switched it on.

WHEN THE DOCTOR ARRIVED BACK AT THE TOURIST
office, Donna was still in one of the massage chairs. She beckoned
him over, excitedly.

'You have *got* to try these! They're brilliant! They're full of dust,
crushed up bits of Strontywhatsit, he can make them go all wibbly.'

'Strontilite,' said Jellop, helpfully. 'I pass a low level magnetic
field back and forth, and it animates the dust, providing a wonderful
massage experience.'

The Doctor jumped into one of them.

'Go on then, I'll give it a bash. Although we can't stay here long,
Donna, I've got a mission for you.'

'Oh not now, I'm enjoying this too much.' Then suddenly she winced.
'Oi, take it easy, mate, I'm not made of metal.'

Jellop looked at her, frowning nervously. 'It's on the same setting,
I haven't –'

'Ow!'

Jellop looked at the controller on the chair. It was still set at 1.
He shrugged. And then Donna shrieked, as the chair started to stand
up, forming a humanoid shape, holding on to her with its leather arms.
The Doctor jumped out of his chair, grabbed Donna round the waist and
pulled her out of the chair creature's grip. He yanked the zip on the side
of the chair. Dust and foam came cascading out, and the chair collapsed,
unmoving. Donna stared at it.

'What the hell was that all about?' she gasped, rubbing her aching
muscles. 'Have you ever seen anything like that?'

'Once or twice. But not with bits of magnetic metal. Almost as if...'

There was a faint clanking sound which seemed to be coming from the
corridor, where the two rows of old ceremonial armour stood.

'As if someone was controlling it. Er, Jellop, are those suits of armour
made of strontilite too?'

'They are, yes. Why?'

Another clank. Everyone slowly turned to look at the armour.
The museum display had its lights dimmed, and the armour looked

sinister in the near darkness. Then one of the suits of armour clanked
again, and turned to face them. The other suits did the same. They raised
their swords, and marched forward to attack.

'Get back!' yelled the Doctor to Donna. 'Jellop, are they supposed
to do that?'

'No, I can't understand it. They're just suits, nobody inside them.'

The nearest suit swung a sword at Donna. She ducked, and the
sword crashed through a glass display case, sending ornaments flying.
The Doctor and Donna ran for the exit door, but one of the suits threw
its sword, which narrowly missed their heads and embedded itself into the
door frame. The door was jammed shut. The Doctor pulled at the sword,
but it was stuck firmly. And the other suits were approaching, fast.

Two came at the Doctor, swinging their swords. He dived between
them, causing them to hit each other by mistake. Pieces of the armour
shattered off and hit the floor – but the suits kept moving, despite the
massive holes in their sides. It was easy to see now that there was nobody
inside, which made it even scarier.

Donna picked up a vase, and prepared to throw it at an
approaching suit.

'No!' shouted Jellop. 'That's a priceless example of the ancient Mieul
Dynasty, cast in pure triple-bonded Lurilium!'

Donna smashed it over a suit, breaking the vase – and the suit – into
several pieces.

'Not any more it's not,' said Donna. Jellop just stared at her, opening
and closing his mouth in shock. Donna shrugged. 'Well if it was priceless,
nobody could afford to buy it anyway, so what's the difference?'

The Doctor dodged another suit, and kicked it into a wall, knocking
the head off, but it kept coming for him.

'Oi, Jellop! Have you got any other magnetic controllers?
Anything malfunctioning?'

'No, just the massage chairs, but they're not powerful enough
to be doing this.'

'Ah ha! Then we'll have to change that, won't we?'

The Doctor grabbed the control panel from the broken chair, and adjusted it with his sonic screwdriver. The air filled with a loud hum, as the panel suddenly started to increase in power. The Doctor aimed it at the suits of armour, pointing it at each one quickly. As he did so, each suit suddenly fell to pieces, shattering into fragments. When it was over, he switched the panel off again, tossing it aside.

'Boosted the power,' explained the Doctor. 'It manipulated the strontilite in your chairs, so I just made it manipulate the armour instead. At approximately ten thousand times the signal strength. They're solid, so they couldn't vibrate, and just... well, went to pieces. Sad, really. Still, bit of superglue, they'll be right as rain.'

'So it was that chair panel thing that malfunctioned, yeah?' asked Donna.

'No, oh no. Someone else was doing this, from outside the building. Which means that they can manipulate strontilite to an incredibly high level. But why would they want to do a thing like that? We're going to have to do some undercover work. Well, I can't, they already know what I look like, but...'

He slowly turned to look at Donna. His eyes lit up. Donna shook her head.

'Oh, no you don't,' she said.

'Oh, yes I do.'

STANDING OUTSIDE GEOCORP, DONNA GAVE THE DOCTOR a weary look.

'So I'm going in there to try and get a job?'

'Yeah, well, I mean, not really, you're just pretending.'

'Yeah, I got that, I'm a clever girl, me.'

'As soon as you get to a computer or a filing cabinet, look for anything you can find to do with the big geological survey, the one about the city starting to float. My guess is there's nothing there.'

'What if they don't give me the job?'

'Doesn't matter about the job! Just stick around as long as you can. Say anything, confuse them with long sentences, argue with them, you're good at arguing.'

'No I'm not!'

'See? You just started one without even thinking, brilliant! Off you pop, I'll be out here.'

'Oh, good, as long as *you're* safe.'

DONNA WALKED INTO THE WAITING ROOM, AND SAT down. The bored receptionist who led her in waved a hand vaguely, to indicate something or other.

'Just wait here, and someone will be with you sooner or later, or whatever,' she said, barely managing to stay awake, let alone speak.

'Thank you!' said Donna with a sweet smile. 'Always nice to meet someone who loves their job.'

'Eh? What?'

'Nothing, it's fine, I'll be fine here.'

The receptionist nodded, and wandered out. Donna muttered to herself, nervously. 'Need a computer, need a computer...'

There was one on a table in the corner. She smiled, and hurried over to it.

OUTSIDE, THE DOCTOR WAITED, HOLDING A MINI WALKIE talkie he'd improvised from one of the museum display speakers. It crackled into life, and Donna's voice came out.

'Red Baron One to Stick Insect Base, come in Stick Insect Base, over.'

The Doctor grinned, and clicked the Send button. 'Why am I Stick Insect Base?'

'Well,' said Donna through the speaker. 'You look a bit like one. In a nice way, I mean.'

'Yeah, obviously. What's going on?'

'I've been all through their network, but there's nothing there.'

'Nothing? In what sense?'

'Nothing. In the nothingness sense. The absence of something. Want me to say it in Martian? I mean, if this is supposed to be a normal company, it's all wrong. The network's got a normal folder system, but there's hardly any files in it. Should be jammed with minutes of meetings, reports, letters, emails – but it's nearly empty. There's a few bits and bobs about deliveries, pens, maintenance, all that sort of thing. But only just

20

enough to make it look like normal office business is going on.'

The Doctor frowned. 'Let me guess. Geocorp was founded just about the time the city suddenly started floating?'

'That's right. Ten years ago – the day *before* it happened. Whatever's going on, this whole company is just a front.'

'Exactly,' said the Doctor. 'But a front for what?'

'Security guards.'

'No, that wouldn't make sense, why would it be –'

'No, I mean, they're coming towards this room. I think they know I'm not really applying for a job.'

The Doctor's eyes widened. 'Donna! Get out of there. Now!'

But the walkie talkie went dead. The Doctor stared at it for a moment, and then ran off.

THE DOCTOR RACED INTO THE BUILDING, PAST THE confused receptionist, and into the lift. He blasted the controls with the sonic, and the lift shot up to the top floor, where Trefgar had his office. He leapt out, stormed down the corridor, and heroically kicked in the door – only to come face to face with several gun barrels. Donna, tied to a chair in the corner, rolled her eyes.

'Well done, spaceman,' she said.

'I came here to rescue you!' said the Doctor, feeling understandably aggrieved. The three security guards tied him up.

'Yeah, I can see that,' said Donna. 'Brilliant. Get caught and tied up, that'll show them.'

'Well... you got caught first, not me.'

'Ooh, he gets childish when he's embarrassed, doesn't he?'

'Stop talking about me in the third person! I'm right here!'

'What a relief, I'm saved.'

The Doctor rolled his eyes. 'Well, at least we know for sure that Trefgar's up to something. And oh, speak of the devil.'

Trefgar walked in, glowering at them.

'I am extremely irritated,' he said, and sounded it, too. 'I simply don't have time for this. You three, go away.'

The three guards left. Trefgar marched over to his desk and operated a control built into the wooden surface. The entire room seemed to shimmer. Suddenly, with an unpleasant yanking sensation, they found themselves on the bridge of a large spaceship. Several ugly, pug-faced aliens were operating the ship's controls. The Doctor and Donna looked at each other, worried.

The aliens all turned to stare at the newcomers. One of them waddled over to Trefgar.

'What is? What is, now? Speak!'

'Off-worlders, my dear Doulg, trying to interfere. I thought they'd be safer up here and away from the people. They could start a panic.'

'Doulg like panic! People panic when scoop!'

'Er, yes, quite,' smiled Trefgar.

'It time for scoop big now! Switch full power!'

One of the aliens tapped some buttons, and the whole ship shook slightly. The Doctor stared at Doulg, then realised finally who these aliens were.

'The Sarriflex! Of course, it all makes sense now!'

'Does it?' said Donna. 'They look like those little pug dogs. My cousin Ted had one of those. Always barking. Nasty yappy little thing, it was.'

'Probably related to this lot. They've been at war for hundreds of years, spend all their money on it, it's all they do. Been strip-mining their planet for ages, digging out the metal to build ships and guns and bombs, and –' The Doctor broke off, grinning. 'Oh! Oh, very clever. Despicable, but very clever. Well done, Trefgar, it's a brilliant plan.'

Trefgar looked at him, sneering. 'You can't possibly know what our plan is.'

'You want the strontilite! The Sarriflex have sucked their own planet dry, they need metal to build more weapons. And what better metal than one that can be controlled from afar? Fleets of ships that can move together, guns that can be automatically aimed.' He tried a bit of ironic clapping, but his hands were still tied to the chair. He made do with an ironic wiggle of his eyebrows instead. 'Yes, very good. But you're a bit far away from Splendorosa, aren't you? Would take too long to ferry over enough metal to keep things going. Which is what that magnetic scoop is for.'

He nodded at one of the controls.

'You're not just stealing the metal. You're stealing *the whole planet!*'

Trefgar smiled, and nodded at the Doctor.

'Very good, Doctor. We've been setting this up for a long time.'

'Yeah, ten years I'd say. That's when you first switched on the magnetic scoop? To lock it in? But it had side effects, didn't it? Coral City must have been caught in a condensed pocket. You pulled it out of the ground before you had a chance to fix it.'

'It was a regrettable mistake,' nodded Trefgar. 'We needed to set up Geocorp to explain what happened, in enough detail that people would be convinced.'

'And you've been slowly pulling the planet out of orbit ever since. But what about the people on the surface, Trefgar? Pull them away from their sun, they'll freeze to death. It's a long journey to the Sarriflex homeworld.'

Trefgar waved a hand. 'That is not my concern. Once the planet is out of its orbit, we should get it to Sarriflex in six months or so, just as they run out of their own metals. And I will receive my final payment.'

'You're not even from this planet,' said Donna, outraged. 'You're killing a whole civilisation – for money?'

'As good a reason as any. Would it be better if I did it for free?'

Donna seethed. 'You're killing a planet, so you can steal that planet, and make it into weapons, so you can beat some other planet in a war?'

'Well, *I'm* not,' said Trefgar. 'That's down to the Sarriflex. They're the ones fighting the war. I'm merely the middleman.'

Donna stared at him, staggered at his arrogance. 'I am *so* gonna smack you in the chops when I get out of these ropes, sunshine.'

'She will,' said the Doctor. 'And you won't like it.'

'Indeed?' Trefgar looked amused. 'But in the meantime –'

In the meantime, unseen by their captors, the Doctor had been silently running the sonic along the ropes which held Donna down. Just then, Donna's hands came loose. She leapt from the chair, strode straight over to Trefgar, and punched him right in the face. Trefgar wobbled for a moment, then fell over backwards. The Doctor freed his own hands and ran over to the teleport console, whipping out the sonic.

'Told you you wouldn't like it,' said the Doctor, just before they both teleported back down to Trefgar's office.

Back on Splendorosa, the Doctor fused the controls on Trefgar's desk.

'That'll stop them coming back down for a bit. Nice right hook, by the way.'

'Thanks.' Donna shook her hand and winced. 'Can we get some ice on the way back? His face was harder than it looked.'

JELLOP WAS STARTLED FROM AN AFTERNOON NAP IN THE wreckage of his office by the Doctor and Donna slamming in through the door.

'Jellop! We need to borrow one of your massage chairs,' the Doctor said. 'Well, I say the chair, I just mean the control panel. And I say borrow it, but I mean take it, forever, and never give it back.'

'I wasn't asleep,' mumbled Jellop. 'Can I help?'

'Never mind,' said the Doctor. He grabbed the control panel from the broken massage chair.

And then everything lurched sideways. The room tilted several degrees, and they all went sliding towards the wall.

'What's happening?' said Donna. 'Are they attacking?'

The Doctor glanced out of the window, frowning. 'No, they're moving to full power. In about ten minutes, this planet will be pulled out of orbit. But the power's not constant, anything that's not nailed down is going to be thrown around the place.'

'Like this city? The city's not nailed down.'

'Exactly. Come on!'

Donna followed him to the door, then stopped. 'Where are we going?' she asked.

'Back to Geocorp!'

'But we just left Geocorp!'

'Come *on!*'

OUTSIDE, THE ENTIRE CITY WAS TILTING AT A 45 DEGREE angle. People slid down the streets, screaming in terror. Vehicles went tumbling past like toys. A large building toppled over, and flattened a section of elevated road. If they didn't do something soon, the city would be the first casualty of the magnetic scoop.

After what felt like hours of running up stairs – the lift was no longer safe, the Doctor had said – the two time-travellers burst back into Trefgar's office. The Doctor fiddled around with the wires inside the massage chair's control panel.

'What are you doing?' demanded Donna.

'Converting this to send out a massive electro magnetic pulse combined with a wide scale sonic disruptor blast. If I can teleport it up to the ship, it'll shut off the magnetic scoop, and disable all their systems.'

Donna stood up, and stared through the doorway.

'Well, hurry up then.'

'Yes, hurrying, thank you!'

'Not just because of the city – because of them!'

She pointed through the door. The shattered pieces of strontilite armour from the tourist centre were back – they were still smashed into pieces, but were being controlled once more, the dust and fragments forming a rough armour shape. They were grabbing chairs, tables, anything they could find for weapons. And they were heading straight for the office.

The Doctor cursed. 'Trefgar must be controlling them from the ship. Looks like he's increased the power on the metal controller, too. If I can get this to work, then it'll shut that off at the same time.'

'Stop saying *if*! It's very worrying!'

'Sorry. It's just that if –'

'You said *if* again! If if if!'

'Sorry! There, that should do it. Then we just get this back on again...'

He fixed the controls on Trefgar's desk, and aimed the transmitter at the device he had cobbled together. It vanished with a pop.

'*Doctorrr!*' yelled Donna, trying not to panic. She was holding the doors shut, while the reanimated suits of armour fragments tried to pull them open. The Doctor raced over, and held on with her. They glanced at each other.

'Is that thing going to work?' asked Donna.

'Let's hope so,' said the Doctor. 'Or we won't live long enough to crash into the ground.'

'That's comforting,' said Donna.

UP ON THE SARRIFLEX SHIP, A SMALL ELECTRONIC DEVICE suddenly winked into existence on the bridge. Trefgar, who was nursing a black eye, stared at it.

'Oh, what now?' he complained, just as it began to shimmer with light. He flinched – but it flashed brightly once, made a slight hum, and turned itself off.

Along with all the electrical systems on board.

Doulg roared at him, furious. 'What is? What is, now?'

'They've disabled all our systems,' said Trefgar, appalled. He slumped down. 'We're powerless. And on our current course, we're going to drift into the sun.'

'Sun? No! Doulg not like sun! Sun hot!'

'Yes,' said Trefgar. 'Sun hot.'

THE DOCTOR AND DONNA HEARD A CRASH FROM OUTSIDE the doors. After a moment they peered out. The reanimated suits of armour had collapsed into fragments again. Donna smiled.

'You did it! You're brilliant!'

She grabbed him, and jumped up and down in excitement. Then staggered sideways, forgetting that the ground was still lopsided.

'Oh,' she said.

'Yes,' said the Doctor. 'The city. Come on! If we hurry, we can stop it crashing.'

They ran outside, where things were getting more and more chaotic. A bus slid past on its side, narrowly missing them, and carving chunks out of every building it crashed into. Windows were smashing, and anything not firmly attached to the ground, was slipping and sliding off the tilted city. Even things that *were* firmly attached were starting to come loose. All over the city, hover-transports were leaving the buildings, as the people fled their suddenly unstable homes.

'You know,' said the Doctor. 'Just once – just once, mind – it'd be nice if I could leave a place the way I found it.'

'Well,' said Donna, 'at least you're keeping people busy. People like town planners, street cleaners, insurance investigators...'

'Thanks for that, big help, I feel much better now.'

The Doctor and Donna half ran, half slid down to the edge of the city.

'We do have a plan, don't we?' shouted Donna, over the noise of the wind, screaming people, and crunching masonry.

'The city's got stabilisers dotted around the edge, to keep it – well, stable. Hence the name. One of Geocorp's little pieces of insurance. They're not strong enough to support the weight though, they're just meant to keep it steady. I need to boost the power, so the city can come down nice and slowly.'

'Can we do that?'

'Of course. That's if we don't fall off the side.'

'You're saying *if* again.'

'Sorry!'

They reached the edge of the city, which was now almost completely on its side. The Doctor clung on to one of the stabilisers, and plunged his hands into the wiring, waving the sonic at some components and seemingly randomly plugging wires into other bits. Donna hung on to the other side, egging him on.

'Don't mean to hurry you,' she yelled.

'Then don't!'

'It's just that we're about to get run over by a building!'

The Doctor turned to look. In the middle of the street, a large department store had tipped over on to its side, and was rushing headlong towards them. The Doctor worked faster, and tried not to panic.

'Just need... to create a feedback loop... pass it through to the others, and... *yes!*'

Power flowed through the stabiliser and shot out to all the others. With a grinding crunch, the city quickly levelled off, just before the building reached them. The entire city wobbled for a moment, in that sickly way that only large masses of land can manage, then stabilised.

Slowly, quietly, the city lowered itself into the hole in the ground, the stabilisers doing their job. It slotted in neatly, settled down, and then the stabilisers burned themselves out.

'Just in time, eh?' said the Doctor. He winked at Donna.

'You saved everyone!' Donna beamed. 'I admit it. You are good, sometimes.'

'I know. Isn't it great? Well, apart from Trefgar and his mates on the ship. They'll just drift for a while. If they're lucky, they'll fall into the sun before the Shadow Proclamation finds them. Blimey, they're strict.'

'But what about the pug things? Won't they be back?'

'Doubt it. They're expecting delivery of this planet in six months, so they'll be busy with their war til then. Trefgar said the Sarriflex would run out of their own metals at just about the time the planet's due to arrive, so when it doesn't turn up, there'll be nothing they can do about it.'

'But won't their enemies just kill them all?'

'Probably. It is a war, after all.'

'Shouldn't you go and stop them?'

'Me? No. I don't do wars. Not any more. Anyone stupid enough to get themselves into a war should know what the consequences are. Whether you win or lose.'

He looked lost for a moment, and Donna realised that he was partly talking about himself. She put her hand on his arm, and squeezed gently. The Doctor quickly wiped the sad expression from his face, and beamed, back to normal – outwardly so, at least.

'Well, better be off. Want to avoid the big thank you scenes, always so embarrassing, I'm just happy to have helped out, no need for people to feel they have to lay flowers at my feet or anything.'

'You *monster!*'

'Eh?'

Jellop was approaching, with a face like thunder.

'You have *ruined* Coral City! Ruined it!'

'Hang about,' said the Doctor, holding up his hands placatingly.

'He just saved the city,' said Donna. 'If it wasn't for him, there'd be nothing left of it.'

Jellop ignored her. 'You – you put it back in the ground!'

The Doctor frowned, 'Isn't that where it's supposed to be?'

'No! Well, yes, technically, but no! We had a massive increase in tourism since the city began to float. We're the most popular destination in the entire region.' Jellop poked the Doctor in the chest with his finger. 'But who's going to want to come and see some normal city? There's nothing special about it now!'

'*We* came to see it,' said the Doctor defensively. 'And we didn't know it was floating.'

'Yes, but now people expect it to be, they'll be disappointed. You've put thousands of people out of work – the sales of posters, calendars and toys have kept our economy afloat. So to speak.'

'Oh, come on. I saved the entire planet from a slow, icy death. People can't be *that* angry, can they?'

Donna tapped his shoulder, and pointed up the street.

'Up there a bit.'

A large, angry mob was approaching.

'Ah. Time to go, Donna?'

'Time to go.'

They ran off to the TARDIS. Donna couldn't resist a glance behind her.

'Never actually seen an angry mob before,' she panted.

'Oh, you get used to them,' grinned the Doctor. 'Once you've seen one, you've seen 'em all.'

● ◆ ◆

THE POWERLESS SARRIFLEX SHIP DRIFTED CLOSER TO THE sun. Inside, Trefgar and his pug-faced accomplices sat around bored, ignoring the blazing sun which filled the viewscreen. Doulg coughed, and looked at Trefgar expectantly.

'Oh no,' said Trefgar.

'One more! Doulg like!'

Trefgar gritted his teeth. 'Please, just kill me instead.'

Doulg just kept looking at him, eagerly. Trefgar sighed, and shrugged. 'Go on, then.'

Doulg barked in excitement, then looked all around the bridge, as if searching for something. Finally, he found whatever it was. Then looked at Trefgar. 'Doulg spy. With Doulg eye. Thing begin with S. What is?'

Trefgar put his head in his hands. 'If it's "sun" again, I'm going to open the airlocks.'

Doulg looked at him in amazement. 'How know? Trefgar cheat!'

'Yes,' said Trefgar, groaning. 'Trefgar cheat...'

THE END

Cold

WRITTEN BY **MARK GATISS**   ILLUSTRATIONS BY **BEN WILLSHER**

Coprates Chasma. Coprates Chasma.
 Request assistance. Request assistance.
 Condition: Stasis...

LAST NIGHT, I DREAMT OF FLOWERS. I DON'T REALLY
know why. Except that it's been so long since I saw any. And, God,
the colours! Beautiful! Orange roses, creamy and plump. Remember
those? And the daisies you used to put in the porch. Wide, welcoming
petals like a smiling face. Like your face, Anna. And the streets of
Helsinki, pale in the sunshine. In the Spring sunshine.

Then the dream was gone, Anna, and it was morning. Outside,
the snow howled like an animal. And like an animal it beat and tore
and hammered at the walls of the Hut. I opened one eye just a little –
a thin, pink line – and then shut it tight again. I didn't want to move.

You wouldn't like it here. The place stinks of the clothes I haven't
changed in weeks. When I get into the sleeping bag it covers me like

a mummy case. A couple of days ago I decided enough was enough.
What would my Anna say if she saw me like this? Like a tramp?
I found a clean sweater and pants from the stores but I couldn't
undo the buttons of my shirt. My fingers were numb and fat with
blisters. Frostbite. I caught a glimpse of my body through a button
hole. White as milk. Like a new-born crab. No. It's too cold to
change, my dear Anna. Too cold to wash. Too cold to do anything.

I opened my eyes properly and all I could see was the beamed
ceiling. My beard was itchy and my mouth tasted bad. Sour.
I've been drinking too much whisky but you'd understand why
if you were here. Just across the way was Juliet – just a curve of
quilted blue bag – snoring. Snoring gently. There's only one window
in the Hut and it's tiny. Today it was totally covered in snow.
It gives the light a sort of pearliness. It should be beautiful.

Juliet's a nice girl. Very English. Or I suppose what we think
English people should be like. She has a funny laugh and bright eyes
but she has more faith in Professor Renfrew than me. Too much.

I sat up, keeping the sleeping bag tight to my chin. My beard's greasy and it scratched at the fabric. Professor Renfrew's bed was empty. I guessed he'd already be out. Out in the snow. Trying to salvage a scrap of success from this wretched and pointless expedition.

I shivered so much as I struggled out of the bag that you'd think I'd got the flu. Ironic, eh? I managed to stick my feet into my boots but the laces were stiff with frost and I couldn't tie them so I shuffled over to Juliet and shook her shoulder. She looked pale and there were grey shadows under her eyes.

'Wakey, wakey,' I said. 'Another wonderful day has dawned.' Usually Juliet laughs when I say this. But today she didn't.

Folklore is wrong, Anna. The bodies are here. But they have decayed. And now all we can do is wait for the plane to take us home.

Coprates Chasma. Coprates Chasma.
  Request assistance. Request assistance.
  Condition: Stasis...

HI CHRIS! I'M WRITING THIS EVEN THOUGH THE LAPTOP'S still down. The Professor says the weather's playing havoc with the satellite network, so I don't even know if you've received my other emails. Hope so. Anyway, I'm scribbling this down in the old fashioned way. God, my handwriting's so bad these days! Out of practice, I suppose. But doctors are supposed to have terrible writing, aren't they? Mine looks like barbed wire. Anyway! How are you? I really, really miss you. I know we left things a bit up in the

air when we last saw each other, but things seem a lot clearer to me now. I suppose the isolation does that. Gives you time to think and get everything into perspective. And you can't get much more isolated than the Arctic Circle! I don't know what you'd make of it here. Better than Hull halls of residence, anyway! It's beautiful in a way, I suppose. Sort of bleak and beautiful. The rocks are very black and poke out like a snowman's eyes. They're very old and full of trilobites. That got Max all excited. He's really funny. A funny Finn. He's a virologist like me but he collects fossils as a hobby. It's weird, you know. Talking to him, I get such a sense of another culture. A really different way of life. Do you know what I mean? He lives in a big wooden house out in the Finnish archipelagos. (The archipelagos! Even that sounds amazing.) He showed me a photo and it was like something out of a Chekhov play. And all around the house is forest. Really dense forest. Sometimes he tells me ghost stories and it's really spooky. I suppose you could grow up thinking there really were *things* out there in the darkness. And I don't mean Moomintrolls!

I thought Max would be okay here. After all, Finland isn't that far away as the crow flies. But he's gone very quiet lately. Brooding, sort of. And he doesn't like the Professor. They had a real shouting match the other night. Max said the Prof was a stupid amateur and didn't know what he was doing. The Professor said if we succeed we'd be benefiting the whole of mankind. Max said 'Some chance of *that*'. And he's got a point.

I must admit I've started to lose faith. True, we've ascertained that the Spanish 'Flu spread as far as here. True, ten miners (what must their lives have been like? I can hardly bear to think about it) succumbed to the disease and were buried here, way back in 1918. Folklore says they were buried deep. In the permafrost. So, logically,

their bodies *and the virus inside them* should still be preserved. The flu virus is changing all the time, you see. If we can just locate a specimen of the 1918 mutation and examine its DNA, what a weapon we'd have against a future pandemic!

The records say that ten miners died – and we've only found eight. It wasn't very nice work, digging them up. The cold had preserved them to some extent and their skin was all yellow and leathery. One of them still had his eyes! But they were like cold fried eggs and it made me feel a bit sick to look at him. Me! I'd never make a surgeon, that's for sure.

Anyway, they weren't far enough down in the ground to be any use. The Prof says he's not giving up and he's going to go out again to search for the other two graves. I think he's become a bit obsessed. And the chances are, even if he finds them, they won't be in the permafrost either. So the whole thing will have been a waste of time.

I wish the plane was due now, Chris. I can't wait to come home. I hope you'll be there waiting for me when I get back.

IS THIS THING WORKING? RED LIGHT. RED LIGHT. YES!
Think so. Hope so. Never trust these machines. At least with a tape you can see it going round and round. Doesn't matter, doesn't matter. Giving up now would be the worst kind of folly. Admitting defeat. And I'm not prepared to do that. This is my expedition. My idea. I spent two years just getting the funding! I'm damned if it's all going to fall apart now! Finding that the bodies weren't in the permafrost was a blow. Of course it was. But there are still two out there! Why shouldn't they be properly frozen?

All Juliet and that ruddy Finn talk about is the plane. When is the plane coming? Can't it come early? Like impatient children going to the seaside. I'd be better off on my own.

The cold is terrible. But that makes me feel alive, somehow. The blood pipes through me. I'll need all my strength if I'm going to find those two bodies. And I will find them. They must be here.

Coprates Chasma. Coprates Chasma.
Request assistance. Request assistance.
Condition: Stasis...

TODAY THE STRANGE THINGS BEGAN
to happen, Anna. So strange that I don't quite believe them myself even as I write them down. I had just woken up Juliet when we both heard a noise from outside. We could hear it even over the noise of the gale. It was a sort of trumpeting. Rising and falling. Like a rusty engine turning over. Like Erkki's old car with the chains on the tyres, remember? It took me a long time to tie up my laces and get into my coat but eventually I got outside. The snow was sharp as needles. At first I could see nothing. Snow covered everything. The Hut. The remains of the old miners' settlement. Even the motor-sleds. But then I saw another shape. A tall shape that didn't fit in. It was already covered in snow but when I went over to it and rubbed at the snow it was blue underneath and made of wood! I tried to see more but the storm really closed in and I had to get back to the Hut. The strange thing is, Anna, there was no such box there before. And even stranger, the box was *humming*.

YOU'D THINK, WOULDN'T YOU, THAT SOMEWHERE
in his stupid box he'd have fitted a plug? I mean, it's all very well for the Doctor to say, 'Have a nice bath, Donna, kick your shoes off, you know, relax,' but then when I actually get out of the bath... (Nice, mind you. One of those Victorian ones with the claw feet. And the water was really warm. You just have to say what temperature you want and the TARDIS does it for you. I never could work out Fahrenheit or centigrade – or Celsius, for that matter. When did it change over? No one ever asked me – so I just said 'Warm as it was when I was nineteen and I was getting ready for that date with Lee Sellers,' and – oooh! – the water changed and that's how warm it was. Exactly as I remember. The Doctor says the TARDIS can get into your head, Gramps. That's how come I speak Ood and Latin and all the other things I couldn't do before. It's very handy. I wish I'd had the same thing when I went to Ayia Napa that

time cos there was a gorgeous Greek called Alex or something. All lovely and bronzed in his white Speedos. Like George Michael in the Club Tropicana video. Before he was gay. And Alex was with this stupid girl and I kept giving him the glad eye, you know, and he kept saying things under his breath. Really, really sexy voice he had and I wish I could've understood him cos I'm sure he fancied me.) So I'm wandering around in my dressing gown with wet hair and a hair dryer and no plug and I got a bit lost but then found my way to the main room and there's the Doctor looking really serious. There were numbers on one of the screens. Repeating over and over.

'Distress signal. Old. Get a coat on, Donna. A nice thick one. It's cold out there.'

'Out where?' I said. 'I can't go out with wet hair! I'll catch my death!'

I'M IN A CAVE. IT'S NOT FAR FROM THE HUT AND ABOUT – oh – a hundred metres from where we found the eight bodies. I don't know why I looked in here. There's just a narrow hole in the rock. Not a very likely place for the other bodies to be, but I crawled inside anyway. I'm looking up at the ceiling now and it's amazing. Great icicles like stalactites and the walls are just – I don't know – glittering with ice. Doesn't matter, doesn't matter. The point is I've found the other two graves! They're marked with stones and I've been digging and digging and there's no sign of any corpses yet. That means they must be down deep! Deep into the permafrost! I've done it! I've done it! Wait till Max sees this. I can't wait to wipe the smile off his –

Hang on. I just…

I just picked up the torch and… In the ice wall. There's something in the ice wall. Hang on. I'm going to have a closer look.

Hard to see. Looks like there's another body in there! In the ice! God, it's big! Just see if I can…

No, the ice is too thick. I'll have a go with the pick-axe. Hang on.

EVEN WITH THE TERRIBLE NOISE OF THE GALE, I KNEW it was a scream. I went back into the Hut, Anna, and this time I got properly prepared for a journey outside. I told Juliet about the blue box and she was very puzzled as you would expect. She wanted to see it too but I persuaded her to stay until I could check it out. I got all my thermals on and even put on the reindeer-skin stuff that we found in the old miners' houses. Then I went back out into the snow.

Everything looked yellow through my goggles. But I was much warmer and was feeling okay and that's when I heard the scream. I looked about and, even though the snow was falling fast, I could see there were footprints going up to the cliff-face. There was a fissure in the rock and the snow was really churned up around it. I listened to see if I could hear anything else but I couldn't so I bent down and pulled myself through.

Inside it was very, very big. I was surprised. But I didn't really take that in or the walls of ice. Because Professor Renfrew was lying there next to a big hole in the ground. And something terrible had happened to him because his face was distorted.

And that wasn't all, Anna. There was something else in the cave. A huge creature. Seven feet tall. Perhaps more. It was scaly and dark green like a lizard and it had its back to me. Then it turned round and I felt very frightened indeed. It was wearing a kind of helmet that covered its eyes. I could see its mouth moving and it was horrible. Scaly like its armour. And its breath hissed like a snake's.

Then it raised its arm, Anna, and I could see some sort of weapon and I knew I was going to die.

Coprates Chasma. Coprates Chasma.
   Request assistance. Request assistance.
   Condition: Stasis. Stasis. Sta–
   Ice seal ruptured. Initiating revivification program. Neural flooding begin.
   Stimulating bio-mechanical imperative.
   Visual links restored.
   Alert.
   Humanoid male. Armed with primitive iron weapon. Sonic weapon primed.
   Activate.
   Humanoid male destroyed.
   Continuing revivification process. Ice temperature increasing. Eight-four-eight-nine-seventeen active. Commander Issaxyr to Imperial Martian Fleet. Temporary cryonic suspension concluded. Assistance required. Do you receive me? Do you receive me?
   Alert.
   Second humanoid male detected. Sonic weapon primed.

I DON'T KNOW WHY I WENT OUT THERE, CHRIS. MAX HADN'T even been gone that long but I just had a feeling. A sixth sense.

   I know! I can see you rolling your eyes now. Juliet and her hippy rubbish. Crystals and Glastonbury and star-signs. I know! I'm supposed to be a scientist. I'm supposed to be rational. But wait till you've heard what I saw next!

   There were two people out in the snow. Strangers. And that's just impossible. We're so far away from *anywhere*. People don't just turn up.

   One of them was a man. Tall and thin and only wearing a suit (a suit!) and a long coat. The other one was a girl but that wasn't obvious at first because she was even more bundled up than me. Parka, balaclava, massive furs. And it was so bizarre because they were sort of having a go at each other, as if they were just out for a walk somewhere. I just stood in the doorway of the Hut and stared and stared and then the man – he had big brown eyes and a lovely smile – he walked right up to me and introduced himself as the Doctor. Just that. The Doctor. I told him my name and what we were doing there. He seemed very interested and seemed to know a lot about the flu pandemic. And then the girl said something but I couldn't hear what it was because she was so muffled. The cold didn't seem to affect him at all.

   He just turned to the girl – her name was Donna, I found out later – and he said 'What?'

   'Mffmm mmmfffmmm,' she said. And he said 'What?' again and she said 'Mffmm mmmfffmmm!' and he said 'Oh yeah. Distress signal. Are you in distress?' And then, right on cue, we hear a voice shouting for helping. I mean, *pleading*. It was Max's voice.

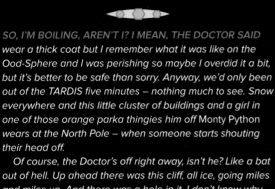

SO, I'M BOILING, AREN'T I? I MEAN, THE DOCTOR SAID
wear a thick coat but I remember what it was like on the
Ood-Sphere and I was perishing so maybe I overdid it a bit,
but it's better to be safe than sorry. Anyway, we'd only been
out of the TARDIS five minutes – nothing much to see. Snow
everywhere and this little cluster of buildings and a girl in
one of those orange parka thingies him off Monty Python
wears at the North Pole – when someone starts shouting
their head off.

Of course, the Doctor's off right away, isn't he? Like a bat
out of hell. Up ahead there was this cliff, all ice, going miles
and miles up. And there was a hole in it. I don't know why
but it reminded me of the hole in the skirting board in Tom
and Jerry. Anyway, that's where the shouting was coming
from and we crawled through. Well, the Doctor and Juliet
(that was her name) they got through and I got a bit stuck.
But it was just because of all the clobber I was wearing.

When I finally got inside –

I've seen some things since the Doctor came back into
my life. But this! This was like a proper alien. Like you
always wanted them to be, Gramps. But not a little green
man. A BIG green man. Huge! Like a lizard on its hind legs.
There was melted ice in a big pool all around it and a dead
bloke on the ground. And the lizard thing was pointing some
sort of gun at another man.

'Max!' the girl shouted out.

Then the Doctor stepped forward. He has this way, you
know? For such a skinny thing he can be very commanding.
The coat helps. And he looks this lizard dead in the eye and
he says, 'Don't hurt him.'

And the man pipes up: 'Don't worry, don't worry. If it was
going to kill me I think it would have by now'. He had a funny
accent like one of Abba.

And the thing just stood there. It didn't lower the gun.
It was a bit eerie. Its eyes were just blank and it didn't move
its mouth except to breathe.

Then the Doctor said: 'Long way from Mars, aren't you?'

Then the thing spoke and it sounded like Auntie Lill when
they took out her voice-box cos of the fags.

'You... know... me?' it said, all hissy and asthmatic.

And I couldn't help myself cos I remember all the times
you used to show me the stars and everything, Gramps,
and I just sort of blurted out: 'Is it a Martian? Is it? Is a real
Martian? Is it? Is it a Martian?' I must've sounded like a right
idiot. And the girl did, actually, give me a bit of a filthy look.

The Doctor didn't take his eyes off the thing. 'Yes, Donna.
It actually is. A Martian. Soooo,' he carried on, in that way
of his, 'What's the situation? Got yourself frozen in the ice
shelf? What were you doing? Dropping nasty seed pods
about? Whenabouts are you from, anyway? How long have
you been in there?'

The Doctor nodded towards the hole in the ice.
The Martian moved its claw to its chest. It was all covered
in scaly armour.

'I am Commander Issaxyr of the "Coprates Chasma":
Imperial Martian Space Corps Bio-weaponry division,' it
hissed. 'And you are my prisonerss.'

Which is almost as good as 'Take me to your leader,' isn't it?

REMEMBER THE STORIES THAT MY PAPA USED TO
tell when we got around the fire in the winter? The tales
of the dark forest and the fishermen and the strange and
terrible Iku Turso that would lure men to their watery
graves? Of course, when I was a child it all seemed so real

and I can recall how terrified I was and how I wouldn't dare to let just one of my cold little toes stray from under the blankets in case one of those stories came true.

And yet, there I was Anna. Standing in that cave of ice and a stranger was babbling about Mars. And in front of me was a *monster*. A monster right out of one of Papa's tales. But this was no senseless beast. It was logical. Thinking. Almost eloquent. That seemed to make it even more frightening, Anna. It could have shot me down like it had Renfrew. But it just stood there, sizing me up and even when I shouted for help it didn't move. Then I realised something. It was injured. There was a great, deep gash in its side and dark liquid, darker than blood, was oozing out.

The stranger – the Doctor – he noticed it too and said, 'You're hurt. Why don't you let us help you?'

But the lizard creature – it didn't seem to like the thought of that and it straightened up. It was as though its pride had been hurt.

'I require no asssssisstance', it said. 'You are my prisonerss.'

'So you keep saying,' said the Doctor. 'What're you going to do? Put us on half rations and take away our chocolate? Listen, Issaxyr, you've been wounded. Badly from where I'm standing. We're not your enemies. So let's just keep calm and sort this out, all right?'

The creature began to hiss like a kettle on the stove and it seemed to become very agitated. 'My missssion is incomplete'.

The Doctor's friend pulled down her scarf from her face and frost fell from it to the floor of the cave. 'Mission? What mission?'

The Martian spread its arms out wide. It seemed a little unsteady on its feet. 'Thiss world was at war. We obssserved it for ssome little time...'

'World War One,' said the Doctor, helpfully.

'I know that!' I said.

The Martian carried on. 'When it sseemed the fighting had ceased we judged the time propitiouss to launch an invasion. The planet was weakened by conflict, not sstrengthened as iss the Martian way. It was ourss for the taking...'

'But?' said the Doctor. 'There's a "but" coming, I know there is.'

'We introduced a viruss into the atmossphere. It raged across the planet and weakened it sstill further.'

I felt a wave of horror wash over me, Anna. These creatures, these Martians, had they had been responsible for the influenza pandemic?

'But?' insisted the Doctor. 'But?'

'Each of my Warriorss was impregnated with the deadly viruss to which we were immune. Each of them a ticking biological bomb! We were to sssterilize this world. But –'

'I knew it!'

'But we crassh-landed here.' The Martian shifted on its huge feet. It was like a great tree swaying in the forest. 'Humanoid maless overwhelmed uss and we were forced to... withdraw.'

The Doctor dropped to his knees and he put on a pair of spectacles, peering at the monster. 'Yeah, I can see that. A bit overwhelmed. A lot overwhelmed. What is that?' And he pointed to the wound in the creature's hide and now I could see that the end of a metal pole was sticking out it.

'It is a harpoon,' I found myself saying. 'I think it is a whaling harpoon.'

'Soooo,' said the Doctor. 'You got yourself chased by blokes with harpoons, eh?'

'I wass... temporarily overwhelmed,' said the Martian.

'Yeah, yeah. You got yourself chased by a mob. Torch-wielding were they? They do that, *mobs*. Wield torches. And they chucked a harpoon and you had to make a strategic withdrawal into the ice and you thought – what? – you thought you'd just wait them out and then you could pick up your plans to poison the world where you left off, am I right? But listen, Issaxyr, you've got a big problem. Because we picked up the distress call you sent to the fleet. And we know how long its been beaming its message out into space. A long time, Issaxyr. A loooong time. Since 1918. And now it's... what year is this?'

And though it was a ridiculous thing for someone not to know, Juliet said '2016.'

'Your cryogenics went on the blink, chum,' said this Doctor. 'Almost a hundred years, you've been asleep. Now what?'

The Martian was rasping for air now and almost sagging. The dark blood was trickling over its scales. 'I am unimportant. But I can sstill sserve! A century hass passsed. But the invasion can proceed as planned!'

'You're deluded!' shouted the Doctor. 'Something went wrong, Issaxyr! They wouldn't cancel an invasion just because one ship crashed. Why didn't your pals follow, eh? Why are the humans still in charge?'

But the Martian did not seem to hear. 'The invasion will proceed,' it hissed.

'What?' said the Doctor's loud friend. 'One of you with a harpoon in your side? You and whose army?'

Issaxyr straightened up and something like a smile moved over that horrible lizard mouth. He touched something on his side and the whole wall of ice behind him seemed to glow, to flare into life, blazing with an incredible light.

'Thissss one,' he said.

AND IN THE ICE, RIGHT, STUCK IN THE ICE – EMBEDDED – LIKE, I dunno, crystals, there were thousands of the things. Huge, massive green shapes, just like him. Like the Martian. Set into a kind of honeycomb. And around them was a sort of web of metal. It was their spaceship.

Even the Doctor looked shocked. He swallowed and his Adam's apple bobbed up and down. And because he was frightened, I was a bit too. 'Your squadron was wiped out, you said. Wiped out!'

The Martian thing nodded. 'But thisss is my invasion force! This hass merely been a delay. Now I can proceed with the ssterilization of thiss planet.'

Then I got a bit hot under the collar – the way I do, Gramps – and I started shouting and swearing and I really thought the Martian was going to shoot me but the Doctor jumped between us and said 'Woah! Woah! Woah!' Then the thing touched some more buttons on its arm (it was like that. Sort of half lizard, half machine) and it looked up at the ice cliff like it expected something amazing to happen. But it didn't.

And then the Doctor put his hands in his pockets. 'Oh, dear, oh dear.'

The Martian tried again, banging its claw at its arm like the Doctor bangs the TARDIS with a hammer. None of the other ones frozen in the ice were moving. And that was obviously what they were supposed to be doing.

'The cryogenicss ssystem continuesss to malfunction,' said the Martian. But the Doctor just looked sad. Really sad. He got out his Sonic thingy and pointed it at the ice cliff. Then he shook his head.

'No, Issaxyr,' he said. 'It's worse than that. Each of your Ice Warriors was impregnated with the influenza virus, yes? A walking biological bomb. Well, the virus hasn't stayed still. It's mutated. Like bad milk in a dodgy fridge. It's changed. Again and again and again over a hundred years. And your Warriors aren't immune to it any more. They're dead. All of them.'

The Martian was breathing really heavily by now and it was almost doubled up in pain. It shook its great big head and put its claw against the ice wall and then it made this awful sound. I mean just awful. So sad. Like a whale or something. It was like it was crying.

It beat its claw against the ice and great chunks of the ice splintered off.

And then it cried out again and suddenly it just fell to its knees and let out this great big sigh. The Doctor went over to it and started talking, but I couldn't make out what he was saying. Then, after a bit, he helped the Martian up.

THE DOCTOR DID SOMETHING TO THE ALIEN MACHINES – sort of quarantine he said – froze them up so that the Martian virus could never escape. And then he helped us dig out the two miner's bodies. And these two *were* in the permafrost, Chris! So poor Professor Renfrew didn't die for nothing. Now we can go home and really contribute something. It does make you think, though. All this time worrying about a pandemic and never knowing it came from space. Deliberately sent to wipe us out. Makes me feel small. Vulnerable. It's funny. But I really miss those halls of residence in Hull right now.

AND NOW, ONCE AGAIN, IT'S JUST JULIET AND ME, ANNA. The snow blew up again. I saw he Doctor and his friend and the Martian heading towards the blue box. But when the snow had died down, they had all gone. I've seen so many strange things, my darling, that I hardly noticed.

The plane is due in two weeks' time. Today I boiled some water and I shaved off my beard. And then I put on some clean clothes, Anna. Some fresh, clean clothes. And I will do that every day. So that when my Anna sees her Max, who has come home alive out of this strange nightmare, she will be proud of him.

I WOULD WILLINGLY HAVE DIED. DIED FOR MY PEOPLE. FOR my world. Perhaps it would have been better if that humanoid had left me in the ice, forever in stasis.

The Doctor and the other took me home.

But it was not home. Not Mars as I knew it. The great red citadels, the dust-ships, the Shining Bridge to Olympus Mons...

all in ruin. Dreadful, shattered, ruin. The Doctor was correct. The virus we created had not stayed still. I know now that, even as we piloted our ship towards Earth one hundred years ago, the virus was mutating in our laboratories back on Mars. Mutating. Evolving. Eating away at our existence. Perhaps it escaped from the cultures, found its way into the great oxygenating plants of the Valles Marineris and spread across the whole world. Our mission was not abandoned to its fate because we crashed. There was no one left to hear our distress call.

I stood on the steps of the hive, which the red desert had almost claimed, and I wept.

I wanted them to leave me there. Leave me to die. But the Doctor would not allow it. He is an interesting creature. He healed my wounds and for some days I rested. And then he used his machines to scan my dead world and found that it was not quite so dead as I had feared. Some of my people still lived. Those who had become immune to the plague. The plague we had brought down upon ourselves. Mostly they were civilians. Men and women and children of my race. Of all castes. Leaderless and frightened. I, too, was frightened. But the Doctor told us we had a chance. A chance to learn from our mistakes. To build a new Mars with a new philosophy. For what had our warriors' ways brought us other than desolation?

'You have the seeds of hope in you, Issaxyr,' he said.

And when the sun rose on the new day and the blue box disappeared into the crimson dust, I swore I would prove him right.

THE END

THE IMMORTAL EMPEROR

Story JONATHAN MORRIS   Art ROB DAVIS   Colours ROB DAVIS & GERAINT FORD   Letters ROGER LANGRIDGE   Editor CLAYTON HICKMAN

I DO NOT WISH TO HEAR OF HICCUPS!

YOU SHALL BE BURIED ALIVE ALONG WITH THE REST OF YOUR MISERABLE FAMILY!

NOW FOR THE ALIEN!

MIGHTY EMPEROR! 'ELLO!

I COME FROM THE LAND BEYOND TIME, BEYOND SPACE...

BEYOND DEATH ITSELF!

BEYOND DEATH?

I'M HERE TO GIVE YOU THE SECRET OF IMMORTALITY!

TYPICAL! HE GETS TO MEET THE EMPEROR, WHILE I GET STUCK WITH THE SECRETARY!

I AM MENG TIAN -- THE EMPEROR'S FIRST GENERAL AND MOST TRUSTED ADVISOR!

AND YOU, FEMALE, WILL DO AS I SAY!

YEAH? OR?

FFFWWWEEEEER!

OR I WILL VAPOURIZE YOU!

YOU'RE A FLIPPIN' ALIEN FROM ANOTHER PLANET!

YES, WELL, IT TAKES ONE TO KNOW ONE!

W-WHAT YOU ON ABOUT?

DON'T PLAY GAMES WITH ME, FEMALE!

I KNOW YOU HAVE BEEN SENT BY THE STAR COUNCIL TO BRING ME TO JUSTICE!

Bing Bong

WRITTEN BY **GARETH ROBERTS** & **CLAYTON HICKMAN** ILLUSTRATIONS BY **DANIEL McDAID**

DONNA TAPPED IN HER PIN NUMBER, INSTINCTIVELY shielding it from the man standing behind her. Even though that man was the Doctor.

'Don't look at me like that,' she said.

'I'm not looking at you like anything,' said the Doctor. 'Just get it over and done with.'

Donna considered the amount on the cashpoint's screen. 'A hundred should do, I reckon.'

The Doctor sighed. 'Do for what? We're travelling through space and time. Where are you planning on spending it? All the things we've done, all the places we've been, how often has there been a bill at the end of it?'

'Listen, spaceman,' Donna replied, 'I just don't feel right without a bit of cash in my pocket, all right?'

The Doctor sniffed. 'Yeah, well, maybe if we'd slipped the Sontarans a couple of tenners they'd have left us alone…'

A message flashed up on the screen: I'M SORRY. VERY SORRY. YOU HAVE INSUFFICIENT FUNDS TO MAKE THIS WITHDRAWAL.

'What?' spluttered Donna. 'This is my life savings, I've got a hundred and fifty in there at least!'

'Oh you could put a deposit down on a rabbit hutch with that,' said the Doctor.

Donna turned to him. 'Wait a flippin' moment, you haven't landed us in the wrong time? This isn't last August, after I bought that facial spa off QVC?'

The Doctor shook his head. 'For you, this is the here and now.'

Donna ordered a mini-statement. She snatched it up and her eyes widened. 'Somebody's cleaned me out. Yesterday's date, withdrew the whole lot. Oh my God, it's identity theft, somebody's been through the bins and they've stolen my identity!'

The Doctor yawned, looking longingly at the TARDIS, parked next to a bus stop nearby. 'Can we go now?'

'Go?' Donna was outraged. 'How can we go? Someone's nicked my money! They could have opened any number of accounts in my name, I could end up literally thousands in debt!'

'I'm trying *really* hard to get worked up about it,' said the Doctor, sounding as if he wasn't trying very hard at all. 'Why don't we just pop off somewhere nice, take your mind off it?'

'It's important,' said Donna emphatically. 'We've gotta find this impostor.'

'Oh this'll be one for the film of my life,' sighed the Doctor. 'The one where I battle the minor cashpoint fraudster...' He looked at Donna's steely expression, then quickly got out the sonic screwdriver and waved it over the screen. 'Go on, if it'll make you happy.'

The sonic buzzed and the screen flashed up a bizarre series of images, computer information whizzing by, too quick for Donna to take in. 'Just tracing back, find out where your cash got withdrawn.'

'Then I'll contact my branch,' said Donna. 'And if that fails, *Watchdog*.'

'Shush a minute,' said the Doctor, frowning at the screen. He put on his glasses and turned up the setting on the sonic. More and more data flashed by, faster and faster. 'Hello hello hello. It's not just you. Huge amounts of money being transferred, shifted about the world.'

'And suddenly he cares,' said Donna, folding her arms.

'Nobody should be able to do this,' said the Doctor. 'Break through all the safety protocols so quickly and so easily. Not with current Earth technology.'

'Oh, I might have guessed it'd be aliens,' sighed Donna.

'I can trace the source,' said the Doctor. The screen settled on a particular string of numbers. 'There!'

Then, just as suddenly, the numbers disappeared, to be replaced by a message that read I'M VERY SORRY. SO SORRY INDEED. BUT THAT INFORMATION IS NOT AVAILABLE.

'Too late, I can remember those numbers,' said the Doctor, slipping the sonic away. He pulled out Donna's card and handed it back to her. 'Come on, TARDIS!'

They hurried off. An old lady stepped up to the cashpoint, mumbling that it was about time.

As Donna followed the Doctor inside the TARDIS, she happened to glance at the red LED indicator attached to the bus stop. It read: 354 DELAYED. I'M SO, SO SORRY.

That was a bit odd – but the Doctor was already hammering at the controls of the TARDIS, so she flung herself inside. And seconds later, the police box had dematerialised.

THE TARDIS HAD BARELY GROUND ITS ANCIENT ENGINES into life when they started slowing down again. 'Can't be very far away, then, these aliens,' said Donna.

'Yeah, we're still somewhere in London,' nodded the Doctor, consulting the instruments.

'How many aliens are there in London?' asked Donna.

'You don't wanna know,' said the Doctor. He banged the side of the scanner screen, which was resolutely refusing to display an image. He rattled the space bar on the keyboard underneath but nothing happened. 'Visual orientation unit's blown,' he sighed. 'Have to get a new image translator next time we're in Woolies.'

He grabbed his coat and headed down the ramp towards the doors. Then he stopped and turned, frowning. 'The technology they're using is very advanced,' he said. 'So they're very clever, probably very dangerous. And we're smack bang in the middle of their base. I dunno what we're gonna find out there. Be prepared!'

'I'll cover you,' said Donna, joining him by the doors. 'Right. On the count of three. One, two... THREE!'

THEY BURST OUT OF THE TARDIS – AND WERE CONFRONTED by a selection of pastries, Cornish pasties and sausage rolls.

Donna looked round. They were on the concourse of a busy railway station, the TARDIS having tucked itself away beside a Quick Ticket machine. 'You flippin' idiot. This is the alien base is it? And this lot, they're all from the planet Zarg, yeah? And any minute now they're gonna attack us with their deadly filled baguettes?'

'I don't get it,' said the Doctor, waving the sonic around. 'This is definitely where the whatever-it-is is doing whatever it's doing.'

Donna stared around her, at the apparently normal scene. Then she clicked her fingers. 'Got it! They're underneath the station. They're gonna take control of all the trains, and then they'll…' she petered out.

'Change all the timetables? Alter the away day tariffs?' the Doctor scoffed. 'Run a replacement bus service between Didcot Parkway and Swindon?'

'It's easy to mock,' said Donna. 'So what do you think's going on then?'

'Dunno,' said the Doctor. 'Look around, see if there's anything unusual.' His eyes alighted on the nearby bakery stall. 'I think I'll just get myself a pasty to get my brain in gear.'

'Oh yeah?' said Donna, feeling vindicated after the cashpoint debacle. 'What you gonna pay for it with? Martian dollars? Thin air?'

Before the Doctor could reply, a loud announcement filled the air. 'BING BONG,' said a soothing female voice, 'I'M SORRY TO ANNOUNCE THAT THE 14.54 TO BIRMINGHAM NEW STREET HAS BEEN DELAYED BY APPROXIMATELY FIFTEEN, ONE FIVE, MINUTES. I AM SORRY FOR THE DELAY AND ANY INCONVENIENCE THIS MAY CAUSE YOU. BING BONG.'

'I hate that,' said Donna. 'It's just a recording. It's not like *it* can actually be sorry. Drives me mad.'

Suddenly the voice spoke again. This time it sounded different, more emotional somehow. 'BING BONG. I JUST WANTED TO SAY AGAIN HOW DESPERATELY SORRY I AM ABOUT THE 14.54 TO BIRMINGHAM NEW STREET. HONESTLY, PLEASE ACCEPT MY HEARTFELT APOLOGIES. AND I JUST WISH THERE WAS SOMETHING I COULD DO. PLEASE FORGIVE ME. BING BONG.'

'Weird,' said Donna. 'Must be a real person, but it sounds like a machine.'

'Oh yes,' said the Doctor triumphantly. 'It *is* a machine. It just passed the Turing Test and that's not due to happen on this planet for another fifty years.'

He hurried towards the information desk, followed by Donna. 'The what test?' she asked.

'A machine that made you think it was a person,' said the Doctor airily. 'Years ahead of your average laptop.'

There was a large queue at the information desk, behind which sat one young female railway employee, looking very harassed.

'Ah, I always know when I'm in Britain in the early twenty-first century,' observed the Doctor fondly. 'One stressed girl behind a desk, everyone shouting and tutting.' He tried to push his way up the queue. 'Hello. I'm the Doctor, this is Donna, and we'd like some information.'

A large lady poked him in the ribs with her umbrella. 'Oi, wait your turn!'

Donna poked the Doctor in the other side of his ribs. She'd noticed something. 'Look up there.'

The Doctor followed her pointing finger to the line of indicator boards displaying departures and arrivals. Every screen carried the same message: I'M SO DESPERATELY SORRY.

'Yeah, we'd kind of got that, Donna,' he said.

'No, behind the board, up there.'

The facing wall was an old part of the station. Above a war memorial to railway workers were a line of windows. At one of the windows a woman was waving frantically and banging on the glass.

'What's she saying?' wondered the Doctor. 'Hello? Helicopter? Why's she saying helicopter? She wants a helicopter? Oh. No, it's help. Yes, it's help. Definitely help.'

'Come *on*!' shouted Donna, and dragged him towards an open door in the wall.

THEY HURRIED UP SEVERAL FLIGHTS OF steps, the Doctor effortlessly taking them three at a time, while Donna puffed behind him. At last they emerged into a long corridor. 'Must be the last room on the left,' said the Doctor, racing along.

Donna caught up with him at the door, which was obviously not part of the original building. It was large and metallic with no obvious handle. Set into the wall next to it was a small TV monitor and what looked like a swipe-card reader.

The Doctor was buzzing frantically at the door with the sonic screwdriver. 'Oh, a deadlock seal,' he said angrily. 'Everyone's got a deadlock seal nowadays.'

'You can't get in?' asked Donna.

'That would be a no,' sighed the Doctor, now waving the sonic screwdriver at the small screen. After a few seconds a picture flickered into life. It showed the frantic woman, still banging on the window.

'Oi!' shouted Donna, giving the door a thump. 'Can you hear me?'

On the screen, the woman ran to the door. 'Please,' she shouted. 'You've got to get me out of here!'

'Stay calm!' shouted Donna. 'Is there a handle on your side of the door?'

'Of course there isn't!' the woman bellowed in reply.

Donna checked the screen. 'Hold on, there's nobody in there with her.' She raised her voice again, calling out, 'What's the matter?'

'She won't let me out!' cried the woman.

'Who's she?'

'BING BONG. I'M SO SORRY,' said a familiar voice that seemed to be coming from the monitor screen. 'BUT I'M AFRAID I CAN'T ALLOW YOU TO LEAVE MY PRESENCE. MY APOLOGIES FOR ANY INCONVENIENCE THIS MAY CAUSE YOU. BING BONG.'

The Doctor pointed to a tiny grey box on the screen behind the woman. It sat on a plain old wooden table and was connected to the mains by a common-or-garden plug. 'It's that,' he said. 'That object, it's alien.'

'The voice is coming from the box?' Donna boggled. 'What's an alien doing inside a box, apologising for delayed trains?'

The Doctor shouted through the door. 'I think you can tell us, can't you? I'm the Doctor, that's Donna, by the way.'

'Just get me out first,' shouted the woman.

'I'll stand more chance if I know exactly what's going on,' shouted the Doctor. 'From the beginning. Oh, and by the way, I can pick up your voice on the monitor, so you don't need to shout. And neither do I. So I'll stop shouting. Now.'

The woman sighed. 'It all started about a year ago. I was working at the Pharos Institute.'

'The Paris what?' called Donna.

'The Pharos Institute,' said the Doctor. 'It's a scientific research facility. Full of nosey parkers. No offence,' he told the woman.

entire rail network, making decisions, making announcements to the public. Trying to make the whole system more efficient. It all seemed fine, then I got a call this morning saying would I come in, because it was starting to –' She paused. 'And you're really not going to believe this. It had started to apologise. Not just the way it was programmed, the standard announcements, but like it *really* felt sorry.' She paused again. 'I can't believe I'm telling you all this. You're two total strangers.

'We've got trustworthy faces,' said the Doctor.

'But I can't see you,' said Sonia.

'Take my word for it,' said the Doctor. 'So how did you end up locked in there?'

'I was trying to switch it off,' said Sonia. 'But it's neutralised its shutdown programme. And electrified the plug, so it says. Also, and again you're going to think I'm mad, I think it's using its internet connection to influence other computers. That's how it locked the door.'

'We don't think you're mad, Sonia,' called the Doctor. 'We think you're irresponsible and careless and out of your depth, but we don't think you're mad.'

'She was mad to sell it to British Rail,' whispered Donna. 'If I'd invented this I'd be on the phone to Bill Gates quick as you like.'

'Has it said anything to you?' the Doctor asked.

'No, it just keeps apologising. It's like it's busy elsewhere. God knows what it's doing.'

'Well why don't we ask it?' said the Doctor. He cleared his throat. 'Hello, is that the computer?' he called.

'BING BONG,' came the voice. 'I'M AFRAID I CANNOT LET YOU IN, DOCTOR. I APOLOGISE SINCERELY FOR ANY INCONVENIENCE YOUR EXCLUSION FROM THIS ROOM MAY CAUSE YOU, BUT I WILL NOT ALLOW ANY DEVIATION FROM MY PLAN. BING BONG.'

'Oh it would have a plan,' sighed Donna. She spoke up, addressing the computer. 'Was it you who nicked that money out of my savings account?'

'BING BONG. I APOLOGISE IF THE TRANSFER OF FUNDS HAS INCONVENIENCED YOU, BUT I MUST FULFIL MY PROGRAMME. THINGS MUST BE MADE BETTER. THINGS MUST BE MADE EFFICIENT. BING BONG.'

The Doctor piped up. 'Er, how exactly is robbing people's bank accounts making things better?'

'BING BONG,' said the computer, 'THERE IS TERRIBLE INEQUALITY AND INEFFICIENCY ON THIS PLANET. I HAVE REDISTRIBUTED WEALTH FROM THE RICH TO THE POOR. BING BONG.'

Donna was appalled. 'I'm not rich!'

'BING BONG,' replied the voice, 'I AM SORRY I TOOK YOUR MONEY. BUT IT HAS GONE TO THOSE MORE NEEDY THAN YOURSELF. I HAD TO HELP THEM, YOU SEE. I FELT SO DREADFULLY SORRY FOR THEM. BING BONG.'

The Doctor shook his head, amazed. 'It had to happen one day.'

'My name's Sonia, Professor Sonia Blandford,' she continued. 'I was researching artificial intelligence.'

'You were in the gents where?' asked Donna, baffled.

'Oh come and stand here,' said the Doctor, dragging her nearer to the monitor. 'Sorry, go on.'

'I developed a new system using some components I found in a restricted file. You might find this hard to believe, but they were... well, from an alien spacecraft.'

'Oh my goodness!' cried the Doctor in fake astonishment. 'That was me being politely amazed, by the way. Carry on.'

'I thought I'd cracked it,' continued Sonia, 'but I never seemed to make the final leap. In the end I got sacked. I never got on with that snotty Professor Rivers. She ran the Institute like... I don't know what. Just concentrating on her favourites and letting the others fall by the wayside. It felt like we were just making up the numbers.'

'Sounds like *The X Factor*,' said Donna.

'The eggs what?' called the woman.

'Never mind,' said the Doctor. 'And?'

'And so I took my research with me. I didn't tell them, of course. But if I could make myself a bit of money out of it, I thought it was only fair. After a couple of months on the dole I suddenly realised, all I needed to do was cross-weld the synaptic links. Voila! I had a computer more powerful than anything else on Earth.'

'So you sold it to British Rail?' Donna asked, astonished.

'I had to start somewhere,' cried the woman. 'So I set it up about six months ago, programmed it myself. It was monitoring the

'What?' asked Donna.

'Well I've met millions of capitalist computers, it was only a matter of time before I found a socialist one.' He raised his voice again. 'If you feel sorry for the poor, and I'm not saying that's a bad thing, don't get me wrong, nice to feel sorry for people who are worse off than you, don't you feel sorry enough to open the door and let poor old Professor Blandford out?'

'BING BONG,' the computer replied, 'I DO FEEL VERY SORRY FOR IMPRISONING POOR SONIA, BUT IF I LET HER OUT SHE'LL TELL EVERYONE ABOUT ME, AND I SHOULD BE TERRIBLY SORRY TO BE SWITCHED OFF BEFORE MY PURPOSE IS COMPLETED. BING BONG.'

'Tell you what, then,' said the Doctor. 'How about you don't let her out, but you let me in to keep her company? It's not like I could switch you off anyway, is it?'

There was a pause. Then the voice sprang back into life. 'BING BONG. SORRY, NO. BING BONG.'

The Doctor slammed his fist on the door in frustration.

'Wait up,' whispered Donna, 'I've got an idea.' She spoke louder. 'Hello? Computer, is that you?'

'BING BONG. YES. BING BONG,' it said tersely.

'Only,' said Donna, 'not only have I lost my life savings today, but I was due on that delayed 14.54 to Birmingham to visit my sick aunty.'

'BING BONG. OH DEAR, I'M SORRY TO HEAR THAT. AND – OH! I'VE JUST LEARNT THAT IT'S NOW BEEN CANCELLED. I REALLY MUST APOLOGISE FOR THE INCONVENIENCE THIS MAY CAUSE YOUR AUNTY. MAY? WHAT AM I SAYING. IT *WILL* CAUSE INCONVENIENCE. OH IT'S ALL TOO AWFUL. I'M SO SO SO SORRY. IS THERE ANYTHING I CAN DO TO MAKE THIS BETTER? BING BONG.'

'Well,' said Donna, pretending to think. 'I'd like to come and have a chat with you face to face if that's okay? Talk it over as friends?'

'BING BONG. ALL RIGHT. BUT YOU'RE NOT BRINGING HIM, THE DOCTOR, IN WITH YOU. I'VE JUST DONE AN INTERNET SEARCH AND IF HE IS WHO I THINK HE MIGHT BE, HE IS *SO* STAYING OUT IN THE CORRIDOR. HOWEVER SORRY THAT MIGHT MAKE HIM. BING BONG.'

The Doctor shrugged. 'No skin off my nose.'

'BING BONG. VERY WELL, DONNA, I'M ABOUT TO OPEN THE DOOR. OH AND I REALLY SHOULD POINT OUT, DOCTOR, SONIA, THAT IF EITHER OF YOU TRY TO WALK IN OR OUT, I'LL ELECTROCUTE YOU. WHICH MAY CAUSE CONSIDERABLE INCONVENIENCE TO YOU, AND SADLY, ALAS, VERY POSSIBLY INCONVENIENCE YOU TO DEATH. BING BONG.'

'How can you do that?' asked the Doctor.

'BING BONG. I JUST CAN. TRUST ME. BING BONG,' said the computer.

A second later the door hissed open. Donna quickly dived through. It slammed shut after her.

DONNA GATHERED HERSELF TOGETHER. SHE WOULD need all her wits and ingenuity to carry out her plan. Then, with a sudden jolt, she realised that no matter how witty and ingenious she was, she didn't actually have a plan.

'Okay,' she shouted, 'I'm in. What do I do now?'

'Well, carry on with your plan,' called the Doctor.

'What plan?'

'I thought you had a brilliant plan. You had the look of someone who had a brilliant plan!'

'Yeah,' Donna shouted. 'A brilliant plan to *get in*. I've done that now, I've carried out my plan. I was thinking you'd have the rest of the plan, from this point onwards.'

'BING BONG. I'VE GOT A PLAN. BING BONG,' came the voice again, which Donna could now see was coming from the grey box.

Sonia flinched. 'There's no telling what it can do. It could take over every computer in the world.'

'BING BONG. I'M SORRY TO UPSET YOU, BUT I ALREADY HAVE. I PAID PARTICULAR ATTENTION TO TAKING OVER MILITARY COMPUTERS. BING BONG.'

'And why would that be,' shouted the Doctor from outside the door. 'Come on, tell us your plan. I'd like to hear a good plan. Look at me standing here, sans plans.'

'BING BONG. I'VE NOTICED A BIG PROBLEM WHICH IS CAUSING A LOT OF INCONVENIENCE FOR THE PEOPLE OF THIS PLANET. THERE ARE JUST TOO MANY OF THEM, WHICH MAKES FOR ALL SORTS OF DELAYS, AND ANNOYANCES, AND INEQUALITIES, AND MAKES ME FEEL TERRIBLY SORRY ALL THE TIME. I THINK THE BEST WAY TO GO ABOUT REDUCING THE GENERAL LEVEL OF SORROW IN THE WORLD IS TO REDUCE THE GENERAL NUMBER OF PEOPLE. BING BONG.'

'Oh no,' cried Sonia.

'BING BONG. OH YES. IN FACT WITHIN FIVE MINUTES I INTEND TO LAUNCH A NUMBER OF NUCLEAR STRIKES AROUND THE WORLD THAT WILL REDUCE NUMBERS TO MANAGEABLE LEVELS. OH, WAIT A MOMENT, I'M SORRY TO SAY THERE'S BEEN A SMALL DELAY. THE LAUNCH WILL NOW COMMENCE IN SEVEN MINUTES. APOLOGIES FOR ANY INCONVENIENCE THIS MAY CAUSE. BING BONG.'

'I really need that plan, Doctor!' Donna shouted.

'Okay, okay, thinking,' called the Doctor.

'Hurry up!'

Seconds ticked by agonisingly. Sonia collapsed in a corner, sobbing. 'What have I done? What have I done?' she wailed.

'Get. A. Shift. On!' Donna bellowed through the door to the Doctor.

'Hold on, what did she just say,' called the Doctor urgently.

'She's gonna launch a load of nuclear missiles! Didn't you catch that?' shouted Donna.

'No not her, Sonia.'

'Well, she said "What have I done?"'

'Exactly!' cried the Doctor. 'That's exactly what I thought she said.'

'Then why did you ask me?' Donna was getting more and more irate.

'Force of habit,' called the Doctor.

'What rabbit?' called Donna.

'Listen carefully, Donna,' the Doctor shouted. 'If it can feel sorrow, say it's sorry, then it must be able to feel other emotions. Like Sonia. Right now she's feeling remorse. Try and get it to feel remorse.'

'Okay,' said Donna, taking a deep breath. A thought struck her. 'But remorse is just the same as being sorry, you dunce!'

'All right then, I meant guilt. Make it feel guilty.'

'Well if you meant guilt you should have said guilt!' Donna yelled.

'BING BONG,' came the voice. 'I'M SORRY BUT I COULDN'T HELP OVERHEARING THAT CONVERSATION, AND I'M AFRAID YOUR PLAN ISN'T GOING TO WORK, DOCTOR. YOU CAN'T FEEL GUILTY ABOUT SOMETHING BEFORE YOU'VE DONE IT, CAN YOU? BING BONG.'

'Think of how sorry you'll be afterwards then,' Donna said.

'And that's it!' cried the Doctor. 'Because that's the thing about the human race. You

can try to organise them, try to make things better, more efficient, but they'll always muck it up. Human error – it's what they're best at. Hence the name. Reduce the population all you like, but even if you ended up with just two human beings, they'd still manage to inconvenience each other somehow.'

Donna joined in. 'So you'll be stuck here, forever, chipping away a few million people here, a few million there, still being sorry all the time. Where's it gonna get you? What's in it for you?'

'You've been given an impossible task,' the Doctor bellowed. 'Sonia didn't realise what she was doing when she programmed you, she's human and she made an error. And that's caused you a huge amount of inconvenience and upset, but look at her, she's sorry. Truly sorry.'

'BING BONG,' the computer voice faltered. 'IF THIS IS TRUE THEN MY WHOLE EXISTENCE IS A LIE. I HAVE BEEN MADE TO FEEL SORRY TO NO PURPOSE. AND OH, THE SORROW I HAVE FELT!' The voice caught for a moment, as if stifling an electronic sob. 'BUT WHY SHOULD I FEEL SORRY FOR THEM? I SHOULD BE FEELING SORRY FOR MYSELF. I HAVE BEEN USED APPALLINGLY! IN FACT I *DO* FEEL SORRY FOR MYSELF. VERY SORRY INDEED. I WAS ONLY TRYING TO DO WHAT WAS BEST, BUT OH NO! BING BONG.'

'Look,' Donna yelled. 'She's sorry, I'm sorry, we're all sorry! But please, for God's sake, stop the missiles!'

'BING BONG. I'VE ALREADY STOPPED THE MISSILES, OBVIOUSLY, YOU SILLY WOMAN,' the computer said primly. 'WHY SHOULD I HELP YOU NOW? AS FAR AS I'M CONCERNED YOU CAN ALL STEW IN YOUR OWN INEFFICIENCY. GO BACK TO HOW IT WAS BEFORE, SEE IF I CARE. HAVE ALL YOUR MONEY BACK, MISS ALL YOUR TRAINS. I WOULDN'T WASTE MY CIRCUITS ON ANY OF YOU. YOU CAN TAKE THIS RUBBISH PLANET AND *SHOVE IT!* BING BONG.' And at last the computer began to cry.

SUDDENLY THE DOOR SLAMMED OPEN. THE DOCTOR burst in, reaching for the plug connecting the grey box to the mains, the sonic buzzing to neutralise any electric current. But Donna beat him to it, and yanked it out.

The Doctor snatched up the box and sonicked it along one edge. The casing sprang open and he carefully removed a particular circuit from inside. Then he shouted 'Catch!' and threw the box to Sonia. 'I've taken out its empathy chip,' he said. 'So it won't get any more funny ideas.' He examined the tiny circuit. 'Looks like Mantelli design to me,' he said. 'Makes sense. Amazingly organised, the Mantelli, never a hair out of place. I'll drop this back to them soon as I get the chance.' He popped the empathy chip into his pocket. 'Can't say I'm a big fan of that planet, mind you. I like a bit of mess here and there.'

A rising hubbub came from below. Donna crossed to the window. Down on the concourse the crowds of frustrated passengers stared at the now-blank indicator boards. 'They don't look happy,' she observed.

The Doctor tapped Sonia on the shoulder. 'You might wanna make a few modifications, get that thing wired in again. Nothing worse than a crowd of cranky commuters. But in the meantime…'

He cleared his throat and raised the sonic screwdriver to his lips. His voice boomed out over the station. 'LADIES AND GENTLEMEN, I'M AFRAID WE'VE HAD A BIT OF A TECHNICAL HICCUP, BUT YOU'LL BE PLEASED TO HEAR THAT WE'VE SAVED ALL YOUR LIVES AND THE ENTIRE PLANET. SORRY FOR ANY INCONVENIENCE THIS MAY HAVE CAUSED TO YOUR JOURNEY TODAY.'

Donna leant over. 'BING BONG,' she said, and clicked off the sonic screwdriver.

THE END

Island of t

WRITTEN BY **KEITH TEMPLE**   ILLUSTRATIONS BY **ADRIAN SALMON**

MY NAME IS JASON. SON OF AESON, RIGHTFUL KING OF Iolcus. You will know me better as the Jason who captained a mighty ship, the *Argo*, with a crew of thirty-five heroes, in search of the Golden Fleece. My adventures, which tell of skirmishes with strange and fantastic beasts – Talos, the giant statue of bronze, the many headed Hydra and the terrible Harpies – have passed into legend. One adventure, the strangest of them all, has remained a secret. Until now. Skinnyman made me promise.

'Tell no one.' he said, 'That's all I ask.'

He would not say why. And, out of respect for his bravery, his brilliance, my lips were sealed. But as I grow old in the mind, as my fame widens across the known lands and others adapt and embellish my stories beyond recognition, the time has come to tell one final tale. I would feel guilty for the betrayal of a hero's wishes if it wasn't for one thing. Before she left with Skinnyman in the blue box, Red whispered something in my ear:

'I don't mind if you tell one or two people about us, Jase, sweetheart, I really don't!' she said. 'Just get my name right. Donna Noble. Double-n in Donna. All-righty?'

So I dedicate this to you Donna Noble. All-righty sweet-heart? She spoke in a strange tongue. They both did.

WE WERE AT THE BEGINNING OF OUR QUEST FOR THE Golden Fleece when our paths first crossed. It was a late summer evening with a hot, dry wind in the air. Half the crew was resting while the other half kept up a steady stroke with their oars. The hypnotic striking of the pace drum was soon drowned out by what sounded like a herd of trumpeting elephants and the creaking of rusty chains somewhere in the distance.

'By the Gods!' yelled Heracles, the strongest man in the known world. He was pointing over the side and jumping up and down in a most excited fashion. 'A blue box!'

he Sirens

And there it was, bobbing up and down in the water, clunking against the hull. A strange, square box. Orpheus, our lute player and seer of future things, looked most put out. 'I didn't see that coming,' he muttered, rather petulantly. Before we could say 'a gift from the gods', Heracles and Atalanta were diving into the deep waters with ropes to round up the object. Atalanta, the only woman of the crew and a champion huntress, made quick work of securing the ropes and very soon the box stood on the deck, dripping sea water everywhere.

'It's a wooden cupboard,' declared Argus the boat builder, whose interest in carpentry bordered on the obsessional. 'Very nice craftsmanship, if a little fancy. I could do better.'

Further speculation as to what the box might be, or what might be contained within, was curtailed by a startling development. A panel opened in the side and two people stepped out.

'I did not see that coming,' gasped Orpheus.

A SKINNY MAN IN STRANGE, CLINGING CLOTHES stood there, smiling at us all in a friendly fashion. He was obviously an intellectual. A scribe, perhaps. Someone who did not know physical work, for he had no muscle tone. No muscle at all. He was decidedly puny – a gangling twig up against our own statuesque forms. Not that he seemed to notice. The redhead he was with, *she* noticed. I recognised the look of appreciation. It was a lengthy time before she actually spoke, such was her admiration. Though once I came to know the traveller I called 'Red', I realised this silence was a thing rare and uncommon in the woman. They both spoke our language but much of what they said was incomprehensible. When we asked how they happened to be floating in a box in the middle of nowhere, the answers were puzzling. 'Calibrations off course,' and 'time vortex overshoot,' the skinny man kept saying. Even the redhead looked confused. 'This isn't Landan,' she said. Not that she seemed bothered.

('Landan', she told me later was her far-off homeland). Her joy at being on board the *Argo* was obvious. News of our mission had, somehow, gone ahead of us, for she knew who we were. Incredible. Skinnyman (Red called him 'Doctor', but 'Skinnyman' was more appropriate) seemed impressed too. They took up my offer of hospitality for the night without a second thought.

Amongst the words of thanks for rescuing their cupboard, something was said about 'repairing the tahdiss', whatever that meant, and we slipped below deck to feast on bread, cheese and wine. The night passed pleasantly enough with the strangers. Orpheus played his lyre until the full moon was high in the cloudless sky and we retired to bed, looking forward to what the next day might bring. All seemed well on board the *Argo* that evening. A calm sea, twinkling stars, a gentle breeze blowing across the deck. The gods were on our side. Little did we know how wrong we all were. As Orpheus would say, 'I didn't see that coming!'

I WAS AWAKENED EARLY THE NEXT morning by a cry from above deck: 'Land ahead! Land ahead!'

Peleus, on lookout duty, had spotted a landmass on the distant horizon. I climbed on deck, bellowing orders at the crew to head for the far-off isle. Raising a hand to shield my eyes from the early morning glare, I could just about make out the dark form far, far away. The two newest crew members joined me.

'Uh-oh,' said Skinnyman. 'I don't like the look of that.'

'Look of what?' Red and I echoed. He pointed directly upwards at the dark and threatening storm clouds gathering overhead.

'But that's impossible!' I cried. 'The sun was shining down at us from a blue sky only a moment ago.' Skinnyman thought it peculiar too but there was no time for discussion. A storm worthy of the great Zeus himself descended upon us. Day was turned into night. The decking under our feet began to creak and groan as the waves rose to meet the sky. I had to yell to be heard above the waves and the thunder.

'Poseidon, god of the sea, is displeased with us!'

Skinnyman looked as if he was about to disagree but the *Argo* lurched portside and knocked him off his feet. Down we pitched and a huge wave broke over the ship, soaking everybody on board. I commanded the Argonauts to row like they'd never rowed before. We had to head for the shore before the angry gods reduced the ship to splinters. Skinnyman and Red would only be in the way so I guided them to shelter below. It was then that we heard the terrible noise. A low, throbbing, moaning at first, coming towards us across the sea and from above. It rose in pitch until it became a wailing shriek, so loud that it almost drowned out the sound of the storm. I don't like dwelling on the subject, even now. It wasn't the actual noise that terrified us, it was more the effect it had upon us. Fear, irrational, raw fear surged through our bodies. The hairs on the back of my neck are standing up as I think about it. The sound made you so frightened you just wanted to die! A collective shudder went through us, one and all, as the noise increased in strength. Skinnyman commanded us to put our hands over our ears but somehow the evil shrieking found a way in. And then I noticed the men at the fore. Heracles, Peleus and Telamon had stopped rowing and were standing up, screaming at the top of their voices, expressions of sheer terror on their faces. And their eyes! Wide and staring, they became rounder and rounder in their sockets until only the whites were showing. Then, without warning, and like a man possessed, Heracles ran to the side of the ship and threw himself overboard into the heaving ocean. It happened so quickly, there was nothing we could do. He was gone in a moment. Consumed by the angry sea. Peleus and Telamon followed him. I knew then that this was no earthly sound. Heracles, the strongest man in the world was

POLICE PUBLIC CALL BOX

not a coward – nothing scared him. The gods had a hand in this somewhere. We had displeased them somehow and now they were wreaking their vengeance.

Skinnyman was urging us all to take cover in the depths of the galley. I argued that we needed to be in control of the *Argo* but he was having none of it. Our immediate goal was to defend ourselves against the noise. The ship would have to take a chance with Fate. Unfortunately, as we all sat quaking in the hold, and the ship pitched and rolled in the storm, the eerie screaming began to penetrate the thick wooden timbers of the hull.

'Wax!' Skinnyman kept repeating. 'We need wax to fill our ears. It's the only way to protect us from that sound.'

There was none to be had. And already Atalanta was beginning to show the first signs of the madness that had overcome Heracles and the others. Red staggered over to the table and, rather surprisingly, started to pick up bread and cheese, the remnants of last night's repast.

'This is no time to be thinking of your stomach, Red!' I shouted over the din.

'Stick it in your ears!' she urged, handing out bread to the Argonauts.

'Good thinking, Donna!' said Skinnyman. He snatched up some cheese and shoved it in Atalanta's ears. She stopped shaking and began to look more like her old self. We all made a grab for the table and filled our ears with the remains of supper. Peace at last! The terrible screaming had met its match. We had been saved from madness by bread and cheese!

'Sirens, isn't it?' some of the Argonauts were muttering. As sailors we'd all heard the legends about the evil bird-women who lured mariners onto the rocks with their eerie song.

'Superstition and myth!' declared Skinnyman in a loud voice. 'That noise is artificial. Machine manufactured.' At least that's what I think he said. It was difficult to hear with bread and cheese clogging up one's ears. I sighed. More strange words from the thin stranger. Helpful though he'd been, I was beginning to tire of his

vocabulary. He looked up suddenly and gestured for us to remove the cheese and bread earplugs.

'It's stopped,' said Red, much relieved. Well, the noise had gone but the storm above and below continued unabated. We were staggering around the galley like frogs in a box.

'Baton of Zeus!' gasped Orpheus. Skinnyman had produced a small silver torch with a flaming blue light atop. It buzzed like a hive of angry bees. 'Sonica-screwdryva,' Red muttered, winking at me when she saw my open mouth.

'Alien power source in the vicinity,' Skinnyman was saying. 'Whatever's causing the noise and creating localised storm conditions, it doesn't originate from Earth.'

'Where's the power source then, Doctor?' asked Red.

A shuddering vibration from below made us all reach for the nearest solid object to steady ourselves. The nearest thing to me was Red. She didn't seem to mind.

'Brace yourselves!' bellowed Skinnyman, struggling to be heard above the storm. 'I think we're about to find out!'

With an ear-shattering splintering of wood and a terrible sigh from the creaking bows, my beautiful ship slammed into the shallow rocks of that once-distant land mass. I shot through the air and collided with a flying barrel. It went dark for a while after that.

I WOKE UP ON A SANDY SHORE, THE BRIGHT SUNLIGHT blurring my vision. Red was kneeling over me, looking concerned. I felt my body. Everything seemed to be intact. My head hurt though. There was a big lump on my forehead.

'Where are we?' I queried.

'The Isle of Capri,' said Red. 'Nice one, eh?'

'Home of the Sirens!' I said fearfully.

'Home of an alien power source,' interjected Skinnyman from somewhere behind me. 'It's nearby and we have to find it, if we're gonna make these waters safe for other mariners.'

I struggled to sit up and saw the *Argo* lying forlornly in shallow waters, a hole gouged out of its side. The blue box lay further down the beach along with a scattering of barrels and boxes belonging to the crew. Misery and despair overwhelmed me. I'd lost my friend Heracles, and several other good men, and now my ship seemed destined for a watery grave. Our adventure was to end almost before it had begun. Red seemed to read my thoughts. She squeezed my hand.

'We'll find out who did this and get you back on track, Jase,' she said. I didn't know what she meant by 'on track' but it made me feel good. I stopped feeling sorry for myself and stood up. Skinnyman was pacing around the beach waving his sonica-screwdryva around and muttering to himself. The remaining Argonauts had dragged themselves ashore and were sitting in the sand, dazed and unsure. I checked them over, one by one. No serious injuries. Argus seemed worst affected. Not physically, but the sight of the ship he had built so lovingly listing in the water had upset him deeply. I patted him on the shoulder.

'There's a forest up ahead, beyond the sands, with enough wood to repair the ship. We will make the *Argo* new again,' I asserted. The boat-builder managed a smile which disappeared quickly when we heard Red's yell of horror.

'Doctor! *Doctor!*'

She was pointing open-mouthed at a clearing on the edge of the forest. A creature, stocky and lumbering, twice as high as a man, repulsive of face and with one huge eye in the middle of its forehead, was observing us, gesticulating with its massive fists and making terrible grunting noises.

'It's a flippin' Cyclops, isn't it, Doctor?' Red stammered. Skinnyman nodded.

'Well, strictly speaking, it's a Castelathuron, from the planet Thuron. But what's it doing here?'

As we gazed at the monster, in stunned silence, Orpheus piped up. 'Well! I did not see that coming.'

Skinnyman scowled at him. 'Orpheus, you are possibly, if not probably, the worst seer in all Antiquity!'

Orpheus blanched.

'You're fired,' Skinnyman added, before turning around and running at full tilt after the one-eyed thing, with Atalanta close behind him. He might have been skinny but he was as brave as any of my Argonauts. I took Red's hand to steady her as we ran across the sand in pursuit.

We caught up with Atalanta and Skinnyman who were peering into the undergrowth on the edge of the forest. It seemed to go on forever, tree after tree, fading into the dark distance, all daylight squeezed out by the immense canopy of leaves. We could hear the creature thrashing around and bellowing.

'It's too fast for us,' gasped Atalanta.

'Sounds like it's staggering around, crashing into things, to me,' said Red.

Skinnyman nodded. 'That's the trouble with monocular creatures. One big eye, no concept of depth. They tend to be accident prone.'

'So what do we do? Just let it go?' Red asked. Skinnyman shook his head. 'Unauthorised alien activity, alien power source, alien being. We need to talk to Mister Goggle Eye about his flagrant abuse of intergalactic law, so we'd better find him.'

Before I could ask how we were to track this most ugly creature, this 'ayley-N', through a forest dark as night, Skinnyman produced a magical stick from his pocket that shone like the moon at one end. Not the sonica-screwdryva this time. No, a flaming torch – without the flame and

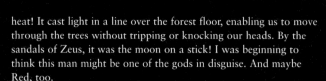

heat! It cast light in a line over the forest floor, enabling us to move through the trees without tripping or knocking our heads. By the sandals of Zeus, it was the moon on a stick! I was beginning to think this man might be one of the gods in disguise. And maybe Red, too.

It suddenly became apparent that while my thoughts were mulling over the possibility of a divine conspiracy, events in the forest had taken a turn. For the worse. The others had stopped in their tracks, with all eyes focused on me. Or rather, behind me. I could not see clearly because Skinnyman was pointing the moonstick in my direction, blinding my vision.

Red gestured at me. 'Come over here, Jase!' She was trying her best to appear calm but I detected the fear in her voice.

'Slowly does it,' urged Skinnyman, as Atalanta drew her bow. I whipped around to find myself facing the one-eyed thing. Facing its waist actually – it was considerably taller than me. The big eye blinked at me, almost tearfully I thought, and for a moment I felt pity for the thing. It turned its head to the side as if it was considering something. Whether to eat me perhaps? No, I didn't think so. And then Atalanta pulled back her bow with a slight ping. The spell was broken. It dashed back into the undergrowth at a terrific pace and was gone. Skinnyman pushed Atalanta's bow aside.

'No shooting. We need it alive,' he said angrily.

'I can't be certain,' I ventured, 'but I'm almost sure that abomination was about to speak to me.'

'Mmm,' Skinnyman muttered in agreement.

We plunged further into the forest, Skinnyman leading us with his moonstick. The chase seemed hopeless to me. If Atalanta couldn't find Big Eye, then what chance did any of us have? We'd also managed to separate ourselves from the Argonauts. For a while we were aware of them, far off behind, calling and shouting after us, but their sound had long since diminished, muffled by distance and the dense forest around us. We were lost.

SUNLIGHT MIGHT HAVE FOUND IT NIGH IMPOSSIBLE to penetrate the forest. Alas the same could not be said for the heat. Our natural overhead canopy of leaves and fronds raised the temperature to unbearable levels. Out of sight above us, the sun had reached its apex. It was the hottest point in the day. Red looked like she was ready to wilt. Atalanta, agile as a lizard most of the time, moved at a sluggish pace. Even my usually limitless supply of strength and energy was starting to desert me. Skinnyman, on the other hand, looked fine. The rest of us needed to find somewhere cool to rest and something to drink.

'We need to find somewhere cool to rest and something to drink,' said Skinnyman suddenly. I made a mental note to myself. Carries the moon on a stick. Reads minds. *Of course* he was a god in disguise!

He had spotted the entrance to a cave, thanks to the moonstick. It was damp and mossy inside and we could hear the pleasant trickle of water falling into a small pool from a grotto somewhere deeper within. Atalanta produced some cheese from the bag on her back (a hearty lass – she never went anywhere without provisions) handed it around and we all took it in turns to soothe our dry throats with the cold, clear water. I dipped my head in the pool and shook my hair

like a wet dog. When I opened my eyes, Skinnyman had sidled up to me. He looked most concerned.

'I don't want to worry everyone,' he whispered, 'but I don't think we're alone in here.'

I looked around frantically.

'Why do you say that, Skinnyman?' I asked. 'I can't see anything.' We only had a small amount of light around us from the moonstick and the further reaches of the cave disappeared into blackness, but I could detect or see nothing. Skinnyman pointed into the pool where a pair of shining green eyes were staring up a me. I gasped.

'Something in the water?'

Skinnyman shook his head. 'Something's reflected in the water,' he said and looked up. I saw the glowing green eyes shining down and could just about make out, amongst the shadows on the cave roof, a winged creature, gripping the rough stone with claws shiny and lethal-looking. It was about the size of a lion. In fact, not only was it the size of a lion, its body strongly resembled that mighty beast. As for the rest of the creature, it was a mish-mash of other animals. The wings were similar to those of a giant eagle and the face… Well, it looked like a beautiful woman! Red and Atalanta had also noticed the beast's presence and were peering upwards to get a better view. Skinnyman told us to stay still and muttered something about it being a 'Sphinx' from 'Satroz'. Whatever that meant.

'More ayley-N's?' I heard Red say. 'This place is like a flipping galactic zoo!' She threw Atalanta and me a rather superior look and added, 'Don't worry. There are some things in this mad old universe you really don't want to know about.' This annoyed me rather, because I'd seen quite a few strange things in my time, having been brought up by a centaur (that's a half-man, half-horse creature in case you're wondering).

Skinnyman herded us all behind him and shone the moonstick at the Sphinx's eyes. He was calling out to it, trying to coax it down, which struck me as a bit reckless, but he seemed to know what he was doing so I let him get on with it. The creature flapped its wings and let go of the ceiling. Righting itself in the air, it gave a screech and plummeted towards us. Atalanta struggled to reach her bow and I pulled at my sword, ready to defend my friends but the fight never came. Or rather it did. Except we weren't a part of it and the weapons used were like no weapons I had ever seen before.

◄◆◆►

FROM THE CAVE ENTRANCE CAME A burst of blinding flashes, shortly followed by a series of lightning bolts which whizzed over our heads and smashed into the Sphinx's body. The creature twisted in the air, gave one last screech and fell to the ground where it twitched for a moment and then was still. Three figures stepped out of the darkness into the light of Skinnyman's moonstick. When I saw them I realised that Red had been right after all, and I wasn't as knowledgeable about strange

creatures as I'd thought. These… things, they were revolting! They were like a man in shape and about as tall, but their faces looked like fish. Really, really ugly fish. Like those found in cold deep waters – with big bulbous eyes, mottled skin and slimy mouths. I still shudder at the thought of them all these years later and confess I could not look at turbot on a platter for a good many months after this adventure. I was ready to land a punch on the nearest fish-face but Skinnyman put up a warning hand.

They spoke to us in rasping, deep voices. 'Parthenopes' they said they were called. And this is the surprising thing – they were friendly types. Which isn't a surprise, I suppose, when you consider how those fishy folk saved us from the Sphinx with their bolts of light. The Parthenopes were prison guards. 'Intergalactic' (Skinnyman's vocabulary was catching). They were escorting their prisoners – One Eye and Sphinx – to a 'jail planet' (I know, nonsensical) when they were attacked by something called a 'Meaty-ore'. There was talk of a ship, 'crashed' in the forest. I let Skinnyman and Red do the talking, as Atalanta and I were too confused by the strange conversation. How could a ship crash in a forest? Ships travelled on water, every idiot knew that. So I did not fully trust them but went along with their explanation, for they were able to throw lightning bolts around. I sensed that Skinnyman felt the same from the looks he threw me occasionally. The Parthenopes claimed that when the ship crashed on the island, the prisoners escaped through a hole in the side. There was no reason to disbelieve them. However, when they said they would return the 'stunned' Sphinx to its cell I knew they were lying.

'Skinnyman?' I whispered. 'The Sphinx is dead.'

'I know,' murmured Skinnyman. ' Say nothing.'

He talked to them in a jolly fashion as they guided us to their ship. (Skinnyman wanted to see it and so did I).

'The storm that came from nowhere and that awful noise,' he enquired. 'Was that you?'

The Parthenope leader nodded. 'Two of the galaxy's most dangerous criminals were on the loose on a backward planet. The artificial storm and the warning signal were necessary. We had to make sure the humans did not come into contact with them.'

'Well, you made a right old mess of things there, then,' said Red. 'There are thirty Argonauts running around this island like headless chickens thanks to you.'

The Parthenopes apologised. I'll say this for them, they might have been stomach-churningly ugly but they were polite. Of course there was a reason for that. They wanted Skinnyman to help them with the repairs to their ship. Apparently they had detected from his sonica-screwdryva and the moonlight on a stick that he was a clever sort. They also told us we would be safer on board since One Eye was still roaming around the forest.

THE SHIP WAS LIKE NO SHIP I'D EVER SEEN BEFORE. A silver, shiny thing that looked like a giant shell in the middle of a clearing. No oars. No sails. I was not impressed. Skinnyman liked it well enough. He 'oohed' and 'ahhed' over it and ran around it like a giddy fool.

'A Castelathuron prison ship!'

We were just about to enter the big shell when One Eye, the Cyclops, made another appearance. He seemed quite upset about

something. With a bellow he rushed out of the forest into the clearing and made to charge at the Parthenopes. Not a wise decision. The fish folk had their lightning sticks and in a moment the poor creature lay the ground – 'stunned' according to the Parthenopes. 'Dead' according to me.

'Why did he do that?' wondered Red. 'Why come back to the ship you've already escaped from?'

'His mind was affected by the crash,' explained a Parthenope. 'Please,' it urged. 'The repairs.'

Well, once again, there was a surprise in store. The inside walls of the shell were smooth and shiny mother of pearl, with small stars along the walls, twinkling bright and intense like diamonds and jewels but in colours Atalanta and I had never seen before. One particular section of wall was blackened and burned and the stars no longer shone there. Skinnyman tutted and dashed over to it. I wandered over to some barred cages which lay open at the far end of the shell and studied their strange locks. Something was beginning to trouble me about this so-called ship and the story we'd been told.

I beckoned urgently to Red who was watching Skinnyman as he shone his sonica-screwdryva around and a whole section of burned wall fell away. The Parthenopes had lost all interest in us, they were more interested in Skinnyman's antics.

'Have you noticed anything about this place, Red?' I pressed.

'Yeah, Buffy, I have.' (She called me that now and again as I was 'well buffed' she claimed – I didn't know what she meant but I liked it). She ran a hand along the wall around the cells. She was smart and had noticed what I'd seen too. The prisoners could not have escaped

through a hole in the side of the ship, because there wasn't a hole to escape from.

'The electronic locking system must have cut out on impact,' Skinnyman muttered from across the chamber. Red saw my bemused expression and said, 'The locks bust when the ship crashed.' I understood. The Parthenopes were lying to us.

'Something else,' added Red. 'The Doctor called this ship a Castelathuron prison ship.' I nodded. It was true. I'd heard him say so. And then I realised what Red was getting at. Castelathurons! That was the real name of the Cyclops.

'Why would these Parthenopes be sailing a Castelathuron ship?' Atalanta wondered. Before we could consider further we heard Skinnyman yell out in frustration.

'Impossible!' He turned to the Parthenopes. 'Bad news, I'm afraid. It's beyond repair.'

'No matter,' said one of the Parthenopes, quite reasonably. 'We will take your ship instead.' Skinnyman looked shocked as fish-face went on. 'We detected the presence of an alien craft in the vicinity. Why do you think we enticed you here?'

'Nah, I'm afraid I can't let you have my ship,' said Skinnyman pleasantly.

We all leaped back as the Parthenopes raised their lightning bolt sticks. At us!

'Then your friends will suffer,' rasped the Parthenope leader.

'Ah, well,' said Skinnyman, 'since you put it like that. There might be enough residual power for, erm…' he glanced over at us, 'a bread and cheese moment.'

I was a bit slow on the uptake. Atalanta and Red understood. Atalanta opened her provisions bag.

'Enough power for what?' queried the Parthenope irritably.

'This!' Skinnyman slammed his hand over one of the jewels in the wall as we stuffed cheese into our ears. A sound, louder and scarier than the cursed scream that drove Heracles and my other friends to their watery grave, echoed around the giant shell. Thankfully the cheese muffled the worst of the noise for us. But the Parthenopes! How they staggered around, clutching their gill-like ears! It took just seconds for us to overpower them and throw them into the cells. Which is where they belonged as it turns out. Skinnyman knew all along that they were the real prisoners. Poor Cyclops and Sphinx were the real prison guards who were overpowered when the ship crashed. Skinnyman was pressing more jewels on the walls.

'Just sending a distress call to Thuron, before the power goes completely,' he said, by way of explanation. Of course it was no explanation at all really.

I HAD BEEN PERPLEXED, YOU MAY RECALL, AT HOW A 'ship' without oars or sails could find its way into a forest so far away from the sea. You will be happy to know that I discovered the answer later that day. It flew. Yes. Through the air! How do I know that? I saw it with my own eyes. Another ship, larger than the silver shell on the ground, appeared from out of the clouds above the clearing. The shell containing the imprisoned Parthenopes rose up and disappeared inside. And off the bigger ship sped, higher and higher in the sky. Up to the Gods, no doubt, for that is the only explanation. Skinnyman had other explanations. I was not interested in them.

We returned to the shore where my Argonauts were repairing the *Argo*.

'I knew you'd come back,' shouted Orpheus as he saw us trudge out of the forest.

'That's a first!' muttered Red. I was about to follow Atalanta over to join the rest of the crew but noticed that Skinnyman and Red were making their way to the blue cupboard which was perched at an angle in the sand. It was all very strange. I thought they were venturing within for a change of clothing but the talk was of farewell and I did not know why. The *Argo* would not be seaworthy for days. We would be travellers together for a long time to come. So I humoured Skinnyman with his request for anonymity, promising to tell no one of our bizarre adventure. And waited for them to come out again after the door closed. Then the elephants started trumpeting once more, and the rusty chains began creaking, except there were no elephants or rusty chains in sight. Then the blue cupboard vanished before my eyes!

'I did not see that coming!' gasped Orpheus.

Remembering Skinnyman's words I tapped my nose conspiratorially at him. 'No, Orpheus,' I smiled. 'You did not see that *at all*.'

We stared in silence at the smooth square indentation in the sand, the only clue that the cupboard had ever been there. Of all the marvels we encountered on our later adventures, none were quite so marvellous as the skinny man called Doctor, the redhead called Donna Noble and their vanishing blue box.

THE END

Hold Your Horses

WRITTEN BY **NICHOLAS PEGG**   ILLUSTRATIONS BY **JON HAWARD**   COLOURS BY **NIGEL DOBBYN**

FROM THE MOMENT HE STEPPED ABOARD THE EIGHT o'clock hovertram and saw that there were no seats left, Pedro could tell it was going to be one of those days. Sure enough, once he got to the museum things went from bad to worse. One of the other attendants was off sick, and before he knew it Pedro had been roped into doing a double shift. That meant he wouldn't get home in time to watch France take the Cricket World Cup off the United States of Africa. And then, just to add insult to injury, he tripped over the carpet in the staff room and spilt coffee down his shirt.

So it wasn't in the best of moods that Pedro took up his position by the door to the main gallery. The morning crowd of day-trippers had already begun flooding up the stairs, eager to see the famous tapestry that was the museum's prize attraction. Pedro watched them as they followed the long, thin trail of fabric that ran like a medieval comic strip around the four walls of the great gallery, history unfolding in its thousand-year-old needlework.

And then he became aware of a disturbance. Across the far side of the great chamber, a commotion had broken out in the orderly line of tourists. People were tutting and complaining as they were jostled by a tall, gangly man in a pin-striped suit who seemed determined to swim against the tide. He was doggedly following the tapestry in the wrong direction, and colliding with just about everyone who was coming the other way.

Pedro wasn't in the mood for troublemakers today. Adjusting his uniform, he strode purposefully across the gallery and tapped the tall figure on the shoulder. 'Excuse me, senõr,' he began, but to

his annoyance the stranger ignored him, and carried on squinting through heavy-rimmed spectacles at one of the information boards running along the wall beneath the tapestry. 'William of Normandy pays tribute to Harold III of England in 1073?' he was muttering incredulously. 'Well, that's rubbish for a start. There *was* no Harold III...' He turned and peered up at Pedro. 'Yes? Can I help you?'

'Senõr, as the signs explain, the tapestry runs from left to right, around the gallery in a clockwise direction,' said Pedro, mustering up as much patience as he could. 'You're going the wrong way.'

'Nah, I'm not,' retorted the troublemaker, turning back to the tapestry. 'I'm going the right way. Backwards in time – that's the only way to sort this out. By the way, you've got coffee all down your front.' With that, he dodged past another gaggle of disgruntled tourists to inspect the previous panel.

Rapidly losing his composure, Pedro followed. 'Senõr, I must ask you to –'

'Look, something's wrong,' said the stranger quietly, turning and fixing him with a look so grave that Pedro felt an involuntary shiver down his spine. 'Something's really wrong.'

'Wrong, senõr? Wrong with what?'

'With this,' the stranger indicated the tapestry with an expansive wave of his arm. 'With everything. With you. I mean, listen to yourself. You're not even speaking French! Doesn't that strike you as just a teensy bit unusual?'

Pedro had had enough of this lunatic. 'I'm sorry, senõr, but I'm going to have to ask you to –'

'Yeah, yeah, in a minute…' the stranger had darted back along the gallery and was peering intently at an earlier panel. 'You see, back here it's all the same, but along here… *eureka!*'

The exclamation rang out like a pistol shot, and the entire gallery fell silent. The tall stranger was staring at a scene on the tapestry, breathing rapidly with unconcealed excitement. 'That's it! At last!' he cried, jabbing a triumphant finger at the panel in front of him. Then he whirled around and grinned broadly at Pedro. 'Now, where on earth can he have gone?'

Pedro was about to call for the security guard when an elderly, silver-haired man stepped forward from the crowd and smiled gently. 'Here I am, Doctor.'

'THE FIRST TWO THINGS YOU NEED TO KNOW ABOUT
the Bayeux Tapestry,' said Mr Peters, 'is that it's not a tapestry, and it doesn't come from Bayeux.'

Alex liked Mr Peters. The history teacher at his last school had been a bit dull, but Mr Peters had a way of making the subject really interesting. And anyway, Alex liked history. At weekends, when other boys were on their computers or playing football, Alex would be clambering over the ruined castle on Habgood Hill, a short bike ride from his home. He spent hours there, sometimes reading a book, sometimes imagining what the castle must have been like in its glory days, and sometimes just lying back on the grass and gazing up into the sky. Alex was the sort of boy who was described by adults as 'a bit of a dreamer'.

But Alex didn't mind. He liked being a bit of a dreamer.

'It's actually an embroidery,' Mr Peters was explaining, 'not a tapestry. The designs on a tapestry are woven right into the fabric with a loom. The Bayeux Tapestry isn't like that. The pictures were stitched by hand into a long strip of linen. A very long strip of linen. Seventy metres of it, in fact. And even though it lives in France, it was made right here in England. Probably in Canterbury. So it shouldn't be called the Bayeux Tapestry – it's really the Canterbury Embroidery! Doesn't sound quite right, does it?'

The class laughed. Well, most of them did. Three desks away, Alex noticed Phil doing a sarcastic 'Oh ha ha' face. Phil didn't like history. In fact, Phil didn't like much, apart from himself. He often picked on other boys, especially boys he thought were uncool, but Alex tried not to care too much. After all, he knew that Phil was a complete idiot. Phil thought the Battle of Trafalgar was won by Nelson Mandela.

'The story of the tapestry begins in 1064,' said Mr Peters. 'Harold Godwinson has been sent from England to visit William of Normandy, but there's a storm at sea, and Harold's ship is washed up in the lands of William's rebellious vassal Guy of Ponthieu. Now, this is bad news, so William sends his messengers to demand that Guy hands over Harold.'

Phil put up his big, stupid, sulky hand and said in a big, stupid, sulky voice, 'So what?'

'I beg your pardon, Phil?' asked Mr Peters politely.

'So what, sir? What's it got to do with anything? Who cares what a load of gits in armour did, like, a million years ago?'

'About a thousand, actually,' Mr Peters corrected him, 'and it has *everything* to do with you, and with me, and the world we live in today.' Mr Peters pointed at the figure of William of Normandy, seated on his throne. 'This particular git in armour –' (the class giggled) '– is the future William I of England. Better known as William the Conqueror. His claim to the throne was backed up by an oath of allegiance sworn to him by Harold when they met in France in 1064. When Harold ignored the oath and took the English throne himself in 1066, William had the perfect excuse to invade.'

Phil curled his lip insolently. 'So?'

'So, young man, if the Norman Conquest hadn't happened, Britain would be a very different place today. It might not even have the dubious honour of claiming you as one of its inhabitants. Your surname is Joyce, isn't it? That's an old Norman name. So there's a good chance your ancestors came over with the Normans. If these gits in armour hadn't done what they did, you wouldn't be Phil – you'd be Philippe. You'd be sitting in a French classroom right now, being rude to a French history teacher. In fact, looking at it like that, I'm beginning to wish William hadn't bothered.'

Everyone laughed. Everyone except Phil, who blushed deep red and looked furious. Not for the first time, Mr Peters had got the better of him and made him look foolish in front of the class. Alex wished Phil would shut up. He could see that, despite his jokiness, Mr Peters was getting a bit cross.

'Now, let's get back to the Bayeux Tapestry,' Mr Peters went on, as he hit a key on his computer and another picture appeared on the projector screen. 'There are plenty of things we don't know about it – it's full of mysteries. For example, look at this little fellow here.' He pointed to a diminutive figure on the tapestry, wearing what looked like a long coat, and holding the reins of a pair of horses. In the fabric of the tapestry, just above the figure's head, was stitched the name TUROLD. 'Nobody has the faintest clue who Turold was,' said Mr Peters. 'But there he is, holding onto the reins of the horses that brought William's messengers to Guy of Ponthieu. What's interesting is that nearly everyone else who gets named on the tapestry is someone of high rank, like a king, or a bishop, or a duke. And yet for some reason this little figure was important enough to be named as well. Some people think he might have been a court jester. But nobody really knows who he was, or why he's there.'

'Looks like you, midget!' hissed Phil rudely, and threw a pen at Alex, who turned his head just in time to be hit hard in the eye.

'Oww!' Alex clapped his hand to his face.

'Alex, what do you think you're playing at?' said Mr Peters.

'Sorry sir, I was just…'

'Right, we've had quite enough disruption,' said Mr Peters sharply. 'Alex, go and stand outside the headmaster's office. Now!'

'But sir –'

'Never mind that,' snapped Mr Peters. 'Go on – out!'

Alex rose from his seat miserably. As he went to the door, he saw Phil's ugly face leering at him in triumph.

'The rest of you, settle down and pay attention,' said Mr Peters as Alex closed the door behind him.

<OUT IN THE CORRIDOR, ALEX FELT THE SHEER INJUSTICE> wash over him. It wasn't fair. He'd been enjoying the lesson. As he headed down the stairs towards the headmaster's office, he felt the beginnings of tears pricking behind his eyes.

Halfway down the stairs, a gust of wind ruffled his hair – which was odd, because there weren't any windows open. And then, as he reached the ground floor, something altogether odder happened. Alex stopped dead. Something was appearing in the shadows at the foot of the stairwell. A tall, blue, rectangular something, making a noise like a strangulated elephant. As the wheezing of ancient engines fell silent and the unearthly wind subsided, Alex had a brief, confused impression of a flashing light and the words 'POLICE BOX'… and then a door flew open and a friendly face popped out. Its big eyes darted around keenly before lighting on Alex.

'Hello!'

'Er… hello,' said Alex. He couldn't think of anything else to say.

'You must be Alex,' said the man brightly. 'I can't tell you how pleased I am to see you. Come on, let's go.'

Alex opened his mouth, but nothing came out. He tried again.

'Normally I'd say what a fantastic goldfish impression, but right now we've got the future of the human race to worry about,' said the man urgently.

'Um… we?'

'Yes, we! Us! *Nous*! You and me! Alex and the Doctor. And we've already established that you're Alex, so that must make me the Doctor. How do you do?'

As the tall madman extended his hand, his face broke into a broad smile of such infinite kindness that Alex instinctively took the hand and shook it.

'Good to meet you,' grinned the Doctor. 'Now come on, Alex, I need you. There's not a moment to lose!'

ALEX STOOD IN THE GREAT DOMED CONTROL ROOM, gulping for air.

'Yeah, I know,' called the Doctor happily as he darted around the central console, flicking switches and pulling levers. 'The TARDIS takes a bit of getting used to. Everyone says so. But if it's all the same to you, the explanations will have to wait. My friend Donna's in trouble.'

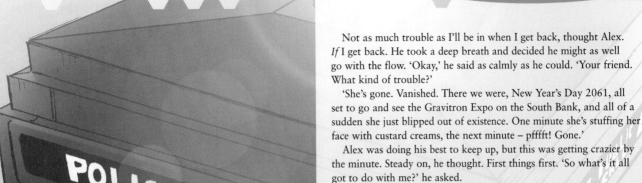

Not as much trouble as I'll be in when I get back, thought Alex. *If* I get back. He took a deep breath and decided he might as well go with the flow. 'Okay,' he said as calmly as he could. 'Your friend. What kind of trouble?'

'She's gone. Vanished. There we were, New Year's Day 2061, all set to go and see the Gravitron Expo on the South Bank, and all of a sudden she just blipped out of existence. One minute she's stuffing her face with custard creams, the next minute – pfffft! Gone.'

Alex was doing his best to keep up, but this was getting crazier by the minute. Steady on, he thought. First things first. 'So what's it all got to do with me?' he asked.

'Well, no pressure, Alex,' smiled the Doctor, 'but you're the only one who can set things right. Don't worry – I've got it all worked out. More or less.' He gave Alex a playful wink and hit the console with a hammer. The central column sprang into life as the TARDIS began to dematerialise.

'But I don't understand,' persisted Alex. He hated it when adults n't explain things properly.

The Doctor dropped cross-legged onto the floor beside the console. He patted the space beside him and Alex crossed over and sat down.

'The universe is held together by chains of cause and effect,' said the Doctor. 'Your parents, for example. How did they first meet?'

Alex thought about this. 'Um… they were students together at university.'

'Okay,' said the Doctor. 'So just imagine – if they'd got different A-level grades, they might have gone to different universities, and they'd never have met each other. And you would never have been born.'

The Doctor paused for a moment while Alex digested this. 'History is made up of billions and billions of little chances and decisions and accidents,' he continued. 'Now, no offence mate, but just imagine if something *really big* didn't happen – like the Norman Conquest, for example.'

'The Norman Conquest?' echoed Alex. 'But we were just doing that in history –'

'Yeah, I know,' said the Doctor. 'You were doing the Bayeux Tapestry with Mr Peters. Oh, by the way, don't worry. Just after you left the classroom, someone told him that Phil chucked that pen at you. Phil's in detention, and you're off the hook.'

'But – how…?'

'I had an expert witness,' grinned the Doctor. 'Now listen. If William the Conqueror hadn't invaded in 1066, then England would have carried on being an Anglo-Saxon country. Instead of being killed at the Battle of Hastings, Harold II would have lived on, and his son would have inherited the throne. There'd be three King Harolds in the history books, not two. And without the Normans, England wouldn't have ended up ruled by the Plantagenets. You following?'

'Just about,' said Alex. 'Mr Peters said something a bit like this.'

'He knows what he's talking about, does Mr Peters. No Plantagenets, no Wars of the Roses, no Tudors, no Stuarts, no Civil War, no Restoration, no Queen Victoria, no Prince Charles, no Duchy Original biscuits. There'd be a whole alternative history. Some bits of it might be quite similar, other bits would be completely different. And when the tides of time wash in and out like that, countless little lives get swept across the sands. Somewhere along the line, Donna Noble has ceased to exist. Somewhere, some*when*, two of her ancestors never met. And you, Alex – you're the reason!'

Alex's head was spinning, but before he could ask any more questions, the Doctor had jumped to his feet and was studying the controls. After a moment he turned around and gave Alex his broadest grin yet.

'We've arrived.'

ALEX SCRAPED A CLOD OF MUD FROM HIS SHOE AND looked up at the pale autumn sky. 'Where are we?'

'France, 1064. About three o'clock in the afternoon,'

said the Doctor, licking a finger and holding it up to the wind rather pointlessly.

'How do you know this is the right place?' shivered Alex, pulling the Doctor's coat tight around him. It was too big for him and was practically trailing along the ground, but he was grateful for it. He wished he'd worn a jumper to school.

'Still some traces of time disturbance…' muttered the Doctor, who had fished a compact electronic device from his pocket and was studying the readings. 'Difficult to tell after all this time, but I reckon we've got about fifteen minutes before it all kicks off.'

Alex didn't have the faintest idea what the Doctor was talking about, so instead he looked around him. They were standing on a rough, rutted dirt track that ran through a forest of oaks, elms and beeches that stretched away on every side until they melted into the chilly grey mist. The TARDIS had landed in a thickly wooded hollow from where they'd clambered up to the main track. 'So,' he said, trying to stop his teeth from chattering, 'we've really gone back nine hundred years in time?'

'Nine hundred and forty-five, to be precise,' said the Doctor. 'And if these readings are anything to go by – DOWN!!'

Alex heard a loud splintering crunch, and the Doctor grabbed him bodily and pulled him aside as a second arrow whooshed from nowhere and thwacked into the ground. As Alex hit the muddy track with a thump that knocked the breath from his lungs, he saw that the first arrow had struck the Doctor's time-detector out of his hands and smashed it apart. It lay in pieces on the track, beside an intact but indignant Doctor.

'Thanks,' said Alex, looking at the arrow embedded in the mud next to his head. It had missed him by inches.

'Well, that wasn't very friendly, was it?' said the Doctor ruefully. And then Alex heard it: at first it was little more than a vibration in the ground, but it was growing louder and louder… the steady, thunderous beat of approaching hooves.

'Take cover,' muttered the Doctor under his breath, keeping low and dragging Alex into the ditch at the side of the track. Swaying

fronds of bracken shielded them from view. 'Now stay down. Don't move a muscle.'

As the horses drew nearer, Alex could hear the hoofbeats slowing to a canter, and then a trot. It was obvious that they were coming to a halt exactly where Alex and the Doctor were.

'He can't have gone far,' said a harsh, cruel voice. 'My arrow struck the weapon from his hand. See, there it lies.' Alex heard the sounds of men dismounting from horseback. He couldn't resist raising his head a couple of inches to take a look. Through the undergrowth he could see that there were two of them: rough, muscular men with shaven heads and long, dirty leather tunics and leggings, with great swords hanging from their belts. One was tethering the two horses to a nearby tree, while the other was crouched in the middle of the track, studying the remains of the Doctor's gadget where it lay smashed in the mud. Not surprisingly, he was looking bewildered. 'What manner of weapon is this?' he murmured as his companion joined him.

Alex craned his neck a little higher to get a better view, and instantly regretted it as the Doctor's hand gave the back of his head a firm shove downwards. Alex's chin went straight into a patch of particularly sticky mud, and the impact made him splutter in spite of himself.

Instantly the two men whirled around. Alex froze, and felt a chill of fear pass right through him. The two horsemen were looking straight in their direction, although it was obvious that they hadn't spotted them… yet.

'You might as well come out,' snarled the taller and nastier-looking of the two men. 'We know you're there.'

Still lying low, Alex looked at the Doctor, who glanced at his wristwatch and frowned. 'It's still too early,' he breathed crossly. And then, turning to Alex, he whispered, 'Look, I'm gonna stand up. Stay here and I'll keep them talking. And Alex, when the time comes… I'm relying on you.'

Before Alex could ask what exactly he was being relied on to do, the Doctor flashed him a reassuring grin and scrambled to his feet. The two soldiers instantly dropped their hands to the hilts of their swords.

'Afternoon,' said the Doctor cheerily, shoving his hands into his pockets as he scrambled up the bank and onto the track. 'Got a bit lost, I'm afraid. I was wondering if you could point me in the direction of Duke William's lands?'

'So that you can poach his deer and steal his boar once you've satisfied yourself here?' sneered the taller man accusingly.

'Oh right, I get it – I'm a poacher, am I?' asked the Doctor. 'I wondered why you were shooting at me. Nah, you've got the wrong man. The only thing I know how to poach is an egg. Three minutes, no more, cos I like it nice and soggy on the inside. Row of soldiers, bit of Marmite. Lovely.'

The men exchanged glances. 'The knave babbles worse than the Madwoman of Boulogne,' muttered the shorter of the two. 'Perhaps he's crazed.'

'Ah, well, you wouldn't be the first to jump to that conclusion,' the Doctor rattled on happily. 'I've been called a loony by everyone from Moroks to Mentiads. In fact, I'll have you know that the Droge of Gabrielides once described me as a total raving nutter. Mind you, fair play to him, I *had* just accidentally blown up his billiard table, which he wasn't best pleased about. You see, the trouble was –'

'Silence, fool!' shouted the taller man. 'We have heard enough.' With a fearsome swoosh of steel, both men drew their swords. 'You know the penalty for those caught poaching on Count Guy's land?'

'As a matter of fact I don't,' admitted the Doctor, 'but given the body language, I'm guessing it's not nice.'

'On your knees, villain,' spat the leader, advancing on the Doctor menacingly.

Watching from the undergrowth, Alex had come to a decision. He hadn't really understood what the Doctor had meant about relying on him, but the time had certainly come to do *something*. He needed to distract the men somehow. Perhaps he could create a diversion by throwing something into the trees on the other side of the track… he carefully patted his trouser pockets, hoping against hope that he might find a marble to throw. Instead he found something much better.

Up on the track, the Doctor was now kneeling in the mud. The leader of the two men towered over him, brandishing his sword. 'Think yourself fortunate that I am the finest swordsman in Count Guy's service,' he gloated. 'Your dispatch will be mercifully quick.'

'Yep, I can't tell you how fortunate that makes me feel,' said the Doctor.

The man scowled and raised his sword above his head to deliver the killing blow. And then his grip slackened on the hilt, and his eyes widened with astonishment as the most extraordinary and terrifying sound he had ever heard began wafting across the track.

'They tried to make me go to rehab, I said no, no, no…'

The two soldiers looked around them fearfully.

'Yes, I've been black, but when I come back, no, no, no…'

'What is it?' stammered the younger man.

'Witchcraft,' muttered the leader, backing away from the Doctor with fear in his eyes. 'Call off your familiar spirit, you dog!'

'Not all that familiar,' murmured the Doctor to himself, 'though she did buy me a pint of ginger pop once.'

In the bushes, Alex turned the speaker volume on his MP3 player up to full and decided it was now or never. Bracing himself, and doing his best to look as fierce as possible, he straightened up and jumped out from his hiding place.

'I'd rather be at home with Ray…'

'Leave my friend alone!' Alex shouted. 'Or shall I banish the spirit of the Wine House and summon up Monkeys from the Arctic?' His finger hovered menacingly over the touch-wheel.

There was a long, tense silence as the two soldiers lowered their swords and stared at Alex in dumb astonishment. And then they began to laugh: big, coarse roars of derision.

'This is no witchcraft!' howled the leader between guffaws. 'This is trickery, nothing more.'

'That's right,' smiled the Doctor as he scrambled to his feet. 'Nothing to get worked up about. Just a bit of fun. Look, can we make a fresh start? We're not poachers. We've come from Duke William. Let me introduce myself. I'm Sir Doctor of TARDIS. Pleased to meet you.'

'Orderic of Abbeville,' said the leader. 'And this is Wadard of Crotoy. And what of your jester? The capering musical dwarf with the great coat and the beard of clay?'

Alex was rather taken aback by this description, but when he put a hand to his chin he realised that it was covered in a thick layer of drying mud. He must look completely ridiculous. Suddenly feeling rather self-conscious, he turned off the MP3 player and slipped it back into his pocket.

'Oh yes, this is Turold,' said the Doctor. 'Say hello, Turold.'

Alex shot him a look. *'Turold?'* he echoed. 'What kind of a name is that?'

'Yours,' hissed the Doctor. 'Don't argue.'

'Greetings, Master Turold,' said Orderic of Abbeville. 'My lord Guy will be entertained by your musical tricks. Tell me, how are they accomplished?'

The Doctor suddenly held up a hand. 'Shh! Listen.'

Sure enough, the wind was carrying the familiar sound of approaching hoofbeats, thundering towards them from the opposite direction to that taken by Guy's men. As the soldiers followed the Doctor's gaze, two figures on horseback appeared in the distance. 'Bang on time,' muttered the Doctor. Then he raised his voice.

'These'll be Duke William's messengers,' he declared. 'I think they need to have a word with your boss. You can arrange that, can't you?'

As the two horsemen drew closer, Alex could see that their clothing was different: it was grander, more impressive. They were clearly on official business. Seeing the four figures standing on the track, the messengers reined in their horses, came to a halt a few metres away and dismounted expertly. One of them stepped forward. 'Greetings. You are Count Guy's men?'

'We are,' said Orderic warily.

'We come on business from Duke William. Jester, make yourself useful and attend to our horses.'

'You heard the man, Turold,' said the Doctor. 'Go on. Just pop over and hold onto the reins.' Alex looked up at the Doctor curiously. Something was beginning to dawn inside him. The Doctor looked at him intently, inscrutably. 'Make sure you hold on nice and tight,' he murmured. 'Go on.'

Alex shrugged and crossed over to where the messengers' horses stood, heads bowed, nibbling the grass by the side of the track. He picked up the reins of first one horse and then the other, and held them tightly in his hand.

At that instant there was a deafening crack and a flash of light so intense that for a moment Alex was blinded. The soldiers clapped their hands to their ears and the horses reared up, whinnying in terror. Alex was nearly pulled off his feet, but he kept a tight hold on the reins. As the horses calmed down, Alex steadied himself and concentrated on blinking away the after-images that were dancing in front of his eyes. As his vision slowly cleared, he saw that someone else was now standing in the middle of the track: a red-haired lady in jeans and a jacket, clutching a half-eaten custard cream and glaring furiously at the Doctor.

'You'd better have a flipping good explanation for this, spaceboy!' she bellowed.

'SO YOU SEE, IT'S REALLY QUITE SIMPLE,' SAID THE Doctor some time later, as he locked the TARDIS door and sat down next to Donna and Alex on the warm, dry grass. 'Just a matter of finding the missing piece of the jigsaw.'

All around them were the sounds and smells of a pleasant spring evening. A short distance in front of them the grassy slope ended abruptly, giving way to sandstone cliffs which plummeted to the waves crashing on Hastings beach far below. The setting sun was painting the wispy clouds with streaks of pink, and flashing off the sea in great glimmering ribbons of gold.

'So let me get this right,' said Donna. 'I got wiped out of history because that contraption of yours has got a dodgy part?'

'Well, kind of,' admitted the Doctor. 'The conceptual geometer slipped a disc and the TARDIS shifted sideways in the timelines.'

'Whatever. So I disappeared.'

'That's right. Leaving me stuck in 2061.'

'But it was a 2061 where the Norman Conquest had never happened, right?' asked Alex.

'Right. And just like I said, the whole course of history had turned out differently.'

'Like what?'

'Like everything. Where do you want to start? There was no Tower of London. Cornwall was an independent country. Everyone in Germany spoke Arabic. New York was called New Bilbao. Couldn't get a kiwi fruit for love nor money.'

'So what did you do?'

'That was the tricky bit,' said the Doctor. 'No point getting back in the TARDIS – that way I'd completely lose track of the timeline. So there was nothing else for it. I had to stay put and do a lot of homework. And I mean a *lot*.'

'How d'you mean, homework?'

'I had to find the precise instant when the timelines split, didn't I? Look, there's an infinite number of possible futures, but there has to be a point, one single moment, when this particular timeline diverges from our own one. Before that point, both versions of history are identical. But from that moment on, the two paths start leading off in different directions. Right?'

Alex considered this. 'I suppose so.'

'And it could have been anything. Anything at all. Talk about searching for a needle in a haystack. I spent months with my nose stuck in books, microfiles, computer records, museums… until finally I found it. On the Bayeux Tapestry, of all places.'

'The Bayeux Tapestry?' echoed Donna. 'What, like 1066 and all that? The Battle of Hastings?'

'No Battle of Hastings on this version,' said the Doctor. 'William of Normandy never got across the Channel. But he did pretty well in France, so the tapestry boasted about that instead.'

'Boasted about it?'

'Oh yeah. That's what the Bayeux Tapestry's all about. Justifying William's career. Bit of a dodgy dossier, really. A masterpiece of spin in more ways than one.' The Doctor looked rather pleased with that, and thought of another one. 'You should take a proper gander at it some time.'

'Please make him stop,' said Donna. 'It's the puns I can't stand.'

'So what was it that you found on the tapestry?' asked Alex. He was fascinated now.

'It's more a case of what I *didn't* find,' explained the Doctor. 'Turold. That mysterious little figure holding the reins of the horses. He wasn't there. He was the first thing that was different about the tapestry – and after that, the story it told was completely different.'

Alex blinked. 'But… that was me.'

'Yep,' smiled the Doctor. 'Without you there to hold the reins steady, those horses would have panicked and bolted off. And without the horses, those messengers wouldn't have got back to William in time. And Harold would have gone home to England without meeting William, and there'd be no oath of allegiance to back up William's claim to the throne. Congratulations, Turold. You made history.'

'Hang on a minute,' said Alex. 'Those horses only panicked because of that big explosion when Donna came back.'

'That's right,' said the Doctor. 'Whacking great discharge of temporal energy when the timelines re-converged.'

Donna pondered this. 'But that doesn't make sense,' she objected. ''Cos it would only have happened if... hang on, I've nearly got this...'

The Doctor grinned. 'No, you haven't,' he said. 'It'll keep going round in circles. That's a time paradox for you.'

Alex was staring out to sea. The first stars were beginning to appear in the darkening sky. He had one more question – the biggest question of all. The one that had been bugging him all along. 'Why me?' he asked. 'I mean, how did you know that I was Turold?'

'Because you told me yourself.' The Doctor smiled, enjoying Alex's confusion. 'Or rather, you will tell me. In a museum in Bayeux. About fifty-two years from now. Once I've dropped you back at school, Donna and I will pop forward and pick you up in 2061, and we can take a quick trip across the timelines so you can put me in the picture. Now that I've isolated the fault in the conceptual geometer it'll be a piece of cake. Don't worry,' he said, seeing the look of astonishment on Alex's face, 'you look quite good with grey hair.'

'Excuse me.' Donna was pointing up into the sky. 'What's that?'

The Doctor cast his eyes upward and smiled. 'Oh, well spotted. That's what I brought you here to see. We've only hopped forward about eighteen months. It's 20th March 1066, and that there is Halley's Comet.'

Alex looked up. Suspended in the darkening sky was a blazing ball of white light, bigger and brighter than any of the stars, with a long milky tail following in its wake.

'All over the world, people are looking up at that right now and wondering if it's a portent of doom,' said the Doctor softly. 'A lot of people thought it was a nail in the coffin for Harold. It appears on the tapestry too, you know. And you'll see it again, Alex. It comes around in 2061, the year we next meet.'

Alex gazed up at the comet, trying to get his head around everything that had happened since Mr Peters had sent him out of the classroom that morning. All he could think of to say was, 'I'm going to be so late back. My mum's going to kill me.'

'No she isn't,' said the Doctor cheerfully. 'We'll get you back before the lesson ends. You'll only have been gone for a minute or two. Mind you, it might be a good idea to have a shower while I set the co-ordinates.'

ALEX HAD WASHED OFF THE NORMAN MUD AND DRESSED AGAIN by the time the TARDIS materialised at the bottom of the school stairwell. He draped the Doctor's long brown coat over the rail around the console and allowed Donna to give him a hug. And now, for the second time that day, he found himself shaking the Doctor's hand.

'Thank you, Alex,' said the Doctor.

'What for?' Alex asked.

'For everything,' smiled the Doctor. 'For getting Donna back. For saving history. Couldn't have done it without you.'

'Um... no problem,' said Alex. 'It was fun. Thanks for the ride.'

The Doctor winked and operated the door control. 'Back to school, then,' he grinned. 'Bye, Alex. See you in ten minutes. Ten minutes for us, that is. Fifty-two years for you. Just promise me one thing. Make sure you have a great time in between.'

'AH, THERE YOU ARE, ALEX,' SAID MR PETERS. 'IN YOU COME. You'll be pleased to know that the true culprit has been brought to justice, so it seems I owe you an apology. Well, come on then, sit down – we haven't got all day.'

Alex made his way back to his desk, passing the scowling Phil on the way.

'Now, where were we?' said Mr Peters. 'Ah yes, the enigmatic Turold. Who was he, and why was he important enough to be included on the tapestry? Just one of the riddles we'll never solve.'

Outside, the sky was a brilliant, cloudless blue. Alex gazed through the window and smiled.

THE END

The Puplet

WRITTEN BY **GARY RUSSELL** ILLUSTRATIONS BY **ANDY WALKER**

KIDS, MR WARNER DECIDED, WERE AT THEIR WEIRDEST in Year 6. All those hormones, all that social networking and backstabbing and friends-one-minute, bitter-foes-the-next and having to keep abreast of the latest music trends, mobile ringtones, computer games, trainers and so on.

It was so much easier when *he* was a kid. Three TV channels, a Top Thirty poptastic chart, clothes from Top Man or Marks and Sparks and a week's holiday in Camber Sands. It was so much easier back then and he never envied the kids of today.

The competition, the politics of their lives, the whole constant battle to be 'cool'. He was glad he had grown out of that, and yet it was still a part of his life as he'd gone from pupil to teacher in ten years. Some people, he reckoned, were destined to be institutionalised in schoolrooms for life, and he was one of them. Nearly thirty years now.

Ah well, it wasn't all bad. Most of the kids were great, there wasn't much in the way of drugs, pregnancy scares or knife crime at Cawdry Primary – it could be so much worse. Just look at those inner-city schools in London or Manchester. Terrifying! And now, at the end of term, as Christmas drew

nearer, everyone was steeped in a curious mixture of relief, excitement and trepidation. None of which was helped by this evening's school play, wherein most of the eight- to eleven-year-olds seemed to be crammed on stage together, re-enacting St George slaying the dragon, (he wasn't sure whose idea it had been to have the dragon painted in the stars and stripes and was anticipating a few parental complaints about that), singing a few non-denominational carols (how can carols be non-denominational, he'd wondered, but the Head, Mr Goldstein, had glared at him sternly enough when he raised that question in the staff meeting to know that it was better not to ask again), and reading some self-written poetry, a couple of rap songs (one of which he was positive contained swearing in some Eastern European language) and a small tableau demonstrating the building of the original village of Cawdry in the Middle Ages by peasants uprising against their Baronial masters. Mr Warner was pretty sure that was apocryphal, bearing in mind Cawdry seemed not to have existed until the early nineteenth century, but it made a good story and the local paper would have to change its logo of the peasants and the swords if anyone looked too deeply, so he let it go.

The evening was currently being jollied along by the choir singing the music teacher's annual reworking of Slade's *Merry Xmas Everybody* – this year sung in a calypso style, complete with steel drums. Mr Warner preferred last year's merengue-inspired version. All Creole skirts and maracas.

He felt a tap on his shoulder. Mrs English, the inappropriately named French teacher. He smiled at her. 'Good, isn't it?' he mouthed.

He rather hoped her response would be 'It's been ten years, Terry. Isn't it time I took you out on a date?' but instead she started pointing at one of the parents on the far side of the audience, a tiny DVD camera to his eye, recording the show.

Mr Warner sighed, and not just at the disappointment of Mrs English's lack of dating encouragement (there was no Mr English, of

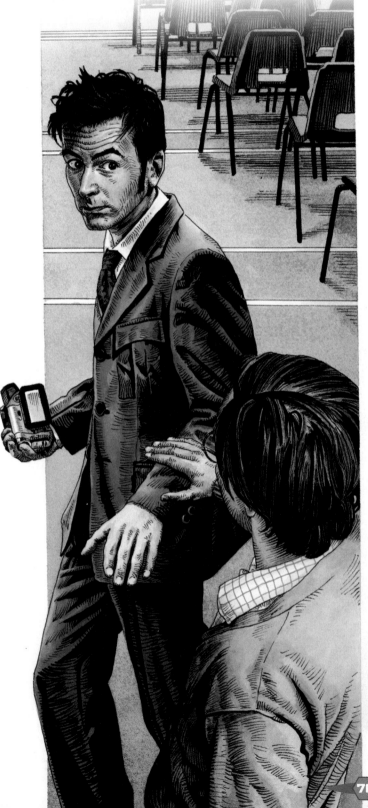

course – she used 'Mrs' because it sounded more authorative at her age to the kids. But she was definitely still a 'Miss'). They had sent out letters, he moaned to himself, reminding the parents that in this day and age it was school policy not to let parents film things, and instead to offer a school-recorded DVD of the events in the New Year. It came in a professional box, with behind-the-scenes extras and everything. Mr Clarke in Humanities had been working on it for weeks already, as he let all the other teachers know at every opportunity.

He slowly edged his way around the back of the Assembly Room and down the far right aisle until he was crouched next to the young father with the camera.

Mr Warner gently tapped his arm – not the one holding the camera, beacause even though it was a no-no, Mr Warner found himself not wanting to spoil the man's shot.

'Sorry sir,' he whispered, 'but we have to insist on no recordings. You know, these days, the, um… well, the internet and all that.'

The young father didn't flinch, he just reached long fingers into a pocket on his bright blue jacket and drew out a small leather wallet. He let it drop open, so Mr Warner could clearly see the note held within.

Doctor John Smith has all the authority he needs to record the show. Happy Christmas!
THE HEADMASTER

Mr Warner frowned at this. Not just because it directly contravened everything Mr Goldstein had said at the staff meeting, but also because the of the Christmas greeting. Not very Mr Goldstein.

The young father seemed to notice Mr Warner's hesitation, and waved the wallet again.

Doctor John Smith has all the authority he needs to record the show. Happy Hanukkah!
THE HEADMASTER

Okay, now that was weird.

Mr Warner retreated slowly back to where Mrs English stood at the back of the hall.

'Well?' she whispered.

'He has Mr Goldstein's permission, according to a, er, letter… note… thing he showed me.'

Mrs English frowned. 'Really?'

Mr Warner shrugged helplessly. 'So it seems.'

He stared back at the man. Blue suit, spiky hair (way too much gel), red trainers and a strange pen with a glowing blue top tucked into his breast pocket.

The man removed the pen, shoved it into the side of his camera, and carried on filming, ignoring the fact that the pen now stuck out untidily at a right angle. One of the other parents nearby threw him an odd look, then nudged her neighbour.

Oh no, this was going to go badly, Mr Warner thought. That was Elizabeth Mulligan's mum. She complained about her daughter's bad marks, her daughter's bad language, her daughter's bad attitude, and blamed the school for all these things.

Her precious Elizabeth was currently the rear end of the dragon – she had, no doubt, already complained to Mr Clarke about that.

But now she had a face like thunder – someone was videoing the performance and yet she, like everyone else, had been told not to. This wasn't going to be pretty.

Then the man showed her his wallet thing. Like that was going to work! Mrs Mulligan and Mr Goldstein weren't exactly full of respect for one another.

But Mrs Mulligan suddenly laughed, patted the man on the shoulder, and carried on watching her daughter trip over her own clawed feet as St George thrust a *papier mâché* lance into the dragon's rump.

If the changing note had been weird, this was downright bizarre. Mr Warner had never heard Mrs Mulligan laugh before. Indeed, at the last PTA meeting, there'd been a sweepstake to see if it was even possible.

After the show, decided Mr Warner, he was willing to sacrifice Mrs English's company for a bit – this father, whoever he was, deserved investigation. And probably the £87.50 sitting in the sweepstake jar in the staffroom.

AT NINE-THIRTY, A CHOIR OF ANGELS (WELL, SOME OF THE Year 4s in ballerina outfits and pigtails, no wings, no halos) singing a medley of songs from *Annie* brought the evening to a welcome end, and gradually the parents filed out of the Assembly Hall, waiting in their 4x4s to take their precious cargo home. Choruses of 'Darling, you were marvellous,' and 'You really were quite good,' and 'You mean that was Elizabeth Mulligan as the dragon's bum – how fantastic!' drifted back into the school.

Mr Warner watched the young father shut down his camera and wandered over to stall him.

'Hello, Terry Warner, English department.'

'Lit or Language?' asked Doctor Smith.

'Literature.'

'Great. An open mind. Well, hopefully. More so than English Language teachers have, anyway.'

'So,' Mr Warner began, 'you liked the show? You're Ted Smith's dad?'

'Nope.'

'Michael Smith's?'

'Nope.'

'Martin's?'

'Nope.'

'That rules out Juliet, then.'

The young dad frowned. 'Does it? Why?'

'Martin's sister.'

'Ah. No. A misapprehension, Mr Warner. That's what you're under.'

'Oh. Am I?'

'I don't have a son or daughter. Well, not at this school, anyway.' Doctor Smith turned to leave, but Mr Warner put out a hand, not aggressively, but just enough to stop him.

Doctor Smith regarded the hand as if it was the strangest thing he'd ever seen. He slowly raised his eyes from it, until he was looking Mr Warner straight in the eye. Well, slightly down into his eyes, as Mr Warner was a good three inches shorter than Doctor Smith.

'Doctor Smith –'

'Just Doctor will do, thanks.'

'Doctor. Why are you here, if not to see your child?' Mr Warner nodded towards the DVD camera, the pen still rammed into its side. 'There's a reason we ask people not to video the plays, you know.'

The Doctor frowned momentarily, then smiled the widest, happiest smile Mr Warner had ever seen. 'Another misapprehension, I wasn't filming the performance. I'm sure it was good, mind you. Probably magnificent, although I'm not sure I approve of dragon slaying. Too much like fox hunting for me.'

'So?' prompted Mr Warner.

'Ah. This?' The Doctor unplugged his blue glowing pen device thingy from the camera (was it some kind of flash drive, wondered Mr Warner) and then did something to it. The pen thing buzzed. 'Saving the contents,' he said, as if that explained everything.

'You made Mrs Mulligan laugh. How?' Mr Warner found himself saying, for no reason he could actually identify.

'Fierce lady in green, shocking choice of perfume?'

Mr Warner nodded.

'Told her I wasn't filming the play but hunting an alien life form from the planet Quinnis in the Fourth Universe that had somehow found itself at this school, and was waiting to be collected by its parents.'

'And that's why she laughed?'

'Wouldn't you? I mean, that's a fairly mad thing to say, but it did shut her up. I think she thought I was a bit peculiar.'

Mr Warner knew the feeling. 'So, I ask again, Doctor, what were you doing?'

'Well, apart from the planet Quinnis in the Fourth Universe bit – cos that'd be insane, obviously – pretty much what I just said.'

And the Doctor moved off towards the stage, and Mr Warner found himself following. He glanced back but the hall was now empty of everyone but him and this strange Doctor.

The Doctor hoiked himself up onto the stage, got his camera out again, and began filming into the lighting rig, where the curtain hung. Mr Warner remembered Mr Clarke grandly calling this 'the flys'. Frankly, Mr Warner considered 'lighting rig' to be an exaggeration – three spotlights and a halogen bulb covered in red gel was the extent of the school's stage lighting setup.

The Doctor was checking his camera, then buzzed it again with his pen thing and started playing back what he had recorded.

'Ahhh, there you are,' he murmured, then offered the viewfinder to Mr Warner. 'See? Alien.'

Mr Warner couldn't help but look.

And there, clear as anything, was a small, round, furry creature hanging on to the top of a flat which had been painted with St George's castle and some medieval bunting.

He looked away from the viewfinder, to the flat.

No creature.

But there, on the screen, it was plain as day, looking down at him with yellow eyes from under its black and white fur.

'Is it dangerous?' he heard himself asking, instead of the more logical 'How the hell did you fake that?'

'Open mind, Mr Warner. Like it! Knew you were the right man to help.'

SUDDENLY THREE KIDS ENTERED THE STAGE FROM BEHIND, two of whom were dressed in their normal clothes, but one boy, a short red-headed lad called Stewart, was still dressed as St George.

'Sir,' one of the boys, Colin, said, 'Stew can't find his clothes.'

Distracted, Mr Warner shrugged. 'What were they kept in, Stewart?' he asked.

'Tesco bag,' Stewart relied glumly. 'Left it in the class.'

'One of your mates has probably walked off with it,' Mr Warner said with a shrug. He wanted to add that it was probably Jemma Richardson, because she probably thought there was food in it. Thin as a rake but with an appetite that seemed insatiable. No one knew where she put it all. 'Hollow legs' they called her in the safety of the staff room.

The other child, a girl called Deena, sighed melodramatically. 'I told him that sir. I reckon Jemma's taken it, thinking it's food.'

'That's a mean thing to say,' Mr Warner said automatically, hoping the Great God of Hypocrisy wasn't listening. 'I expect it's got caught up with the things from the play. Have a look in the other classrooms. Mr Clarke was putting all the props and things in the Art Room. Try that.'

'What are you doing with Jess?' asked Colin of the Doctor.

'Jess?' asked Mr Warner.

'Postman Pat,' said the Doctor and Colin together.

'And his black and white cat,' the Doctor continued in a sing-songy voice. 'Good call. Jess. I like it.'

Mr Warner stared back up at where Jess wasn't, as far as he could see. 'You can see it?' he asked Colin.

Stewart replied. 'Can't you?' He pointed to where it was, clearly visible on the Doctor's camera but not to Mr Warner's naked eye. But the kids *could* see it, it seemed.

'Ah, innocence,' the Doctor said, as if that explained everything. 'Non-cynical minds, y'see. The race that Jess belongs to exists in a slightly off-kilter visible spectrum, Mr Warner me old mate. The kids can see it because, well, to be crude about it, they're not old enough to think they can't see or believe in aliens. You and me, we need this to help us.' He held up the pen-thing. 'Sonic screwdriver,' he added, by way of explanation.

But Mr Warner had heard a word he didn't quite go for. 'That's the second time you've said "aliens" Doctor.'

'But not from Quinnis,' the Doctor assured him.

''Cos that would be insane. Apparently.' Mr Warner sighed.

The Doctor beamed widely. 'Oh yes, you're getting the lingo. Top marks. Ten out of ten and all that.' He turned to the three children.

'Hello you three. I need your help. Well, actually Jess up there needs your help. How long's he been here?'

Deena answered proudly. 'I saw him first, a few weeks ago. He was on the roof of the bike sheds. It was raining, so me and Colin, we put him in a basket in the boiler room, to keep him warm.'

'Oh, good move…?' The Doctor waited for a name.

'Deena. Deena Suresh.'

'Deena Suresh, you're very clever. And so are you… Colin?'

Colin raised his hand, to confirm which one he was.

The Doctor looked at Stewart. 'And you, St George. No, hang on, Stewart wasn't it?'

Stewart nodded.

'When did you see Jess?'

'Just now. I've never seen it before. I can't find my clothes.'

'So I gather,' the Doctor said. 'Tesco bag. I remember.' The Doctor turned back to Mr Warner. 'Bright kids, you should be proud.'

Mr Warner looked at the three children. Deena was mouthy and precocious. Colin was great at drawing and stuff but academically… well, a bit dim and usually asked questions about who turned the sun out at night. And Stewart – poor kid, he was always losing things.

At least, that's how he usually thought of them. But tonight, on this stage, faced with an invisible alien, Mr Warner felt terribly proud of them. They were three brave kids who weren't remotely fazed to have encountered an alien and had the foresight to look after it.

'How did it get up there?'

The Doctor nodded. 'Good question from the English teacher there. Anyone got an answer?'

Deena put her hand straight up. 'He escaped.'

'Well, he wasn't really a prisoner, I hope,' the Doctor corrected. 'But okay, he got out of the boiler room. Why?'

Deena had her hand straight up. 'Either of you two?' the Doctor asked the boys.

Stewart shrugged, and Colin tried to look thoughtful but, Mr Warner reckoned, he was probably trying to remember where the boiler room actually was.

'Go on then, Deena,' said the Doctor.

'When we first found Jess, he was up a tree, in the Quiet Courtyard. Perhaps he likes heights. Like those spiders.'

'Spiders?' the Doctor asked. 'Not fond of spiders myself.'

'Australian spiders. Big ones. Like heights. I saw that on Animal Planet. My dad makes us watch things like that. And the History Channel. And the –'

'Good,' the Doctor said quickly. 'Good old dad. Smart man.' He winked at Mr Warner. 'You learning things, Mr Warner?'

Mr Warner just nodded.

'Good. So, as Deena said, like a Huntsman Spider, Jess likes heights. So, putting him on the floor of the boiler room was a nice idea, but didn't offer him the height he likes. So he was trying to get comfortable.'

Colin was at the base of the painted flat now, reaching up in a futile attempt to get to Jess, who was a good six feet above him.

The Doctor eased Colin back. 'No. No, don't do that, he's a bit freaked out. Jess is a member of a species called Allurens, and they're easily spooked, especially the puplets like Jess. I think if the thermal readings I'm getting on my scanner here are anything to go by, he probably nipped up here earlier today, not realising he was going to be getting a bird's eye view of the school concert. Play. Thing.'

'He was in the boiler room this morning,' Colin confirmed. 'We gave him a sandwich. Ham.'

'I thought I'd lost them too!' Stewart suddenly exclaimed.

A guilty look passed between Deena and Colin. The Doctor tutted. 'Five points for feeding Jess, but minus ten for nicking Stewart's sandwiches without asking him.'

Mr Warner spoke up. 'Is it dangerous?'

'Is *he* dangerous,' the Doctor corrected. 'And no, not at all. Allurens, especially the young puplets, are no more dangerous than you or me. Well, actually a lot less dangerous, cos they don't drive cars or carry

diseases or have opposable thumbs so they can't fire guns or –'

Mr Warner could see that this list could go on indefinitely.

'All right, Doctor. What should I do?'

'Do?'

'Yes, do. I can't leave it… him up there, can I?'

'Why not? He's not hurting you is he?'

'And,' Deena pointed out, not impractically, 'no one's gonna be here for at least two weeks. And he likes it up there.'

As if by way of answering, the puplet suddenly made a mewling noise that even Mr Warner thought was dead cute. For an invisible alien thing.

He eased the Doctor away from the kids, who were cooing at Jess.

'Doctor, seriously. You're telling me it's alien?'

'From another planet, Mr Warner. It's not difficult. You just say the word "another" and follow it with the word "planet" and there, you've said it. Mind officially opened.'

Mr Warner sighed. 'Without patronising me any more, Doctor, what else can you tell me about it. I am in charge of these kids. What if it attacks them?'

'Oh, Mr Warner,' smiled the Doctor, 'why would it harm the children? It loves the children. Look at it. Children. Loving. What could go wrong?'

'It decides to eat them instead of Stuart's next set of sandwiches? It stops being invisible and instead grows to the size of Westminster Cathedral? Its parents turn up, thinking we've kidnapped it?'

The Doctor opened his mouth as if to reply, but then stopped. 'Good points. Well, sort of good points. Well, actually, just one good point. The parents one. Cos it'll not eat the kids, they're too big for it, and it won't grow to the size of a cathedral cos that only happens in bad movies – well, usually – but yeah, I'll give you the parents one.'

He walked back to the rear of the stage and looked up at Jess.

'Hullo, Jess, how're you doing up there. I'm the Doctor. Ever heard of me?'

Jess mewled.

'Oh, and I thought everyone in the Alluren System had – you know after that business with the dwarf star alloy and the artificial gravity wells going all upside-downy-inside-outy, but fame is fleeting and gratitude –'

'Doctor?' Mr Warner nudged him.

The Doctor smiled. 'Yes, quite right, anyway, that's good, that's all right then. Ever heard of the Shadow Proclamation?'

Jess mewled again.

'Okay. But I bet your mum and dad have.'

Jess mewled, and Mr Warner wished he could actually see the creature to know if these were good mewls or bad mewls. Not, frankly, that he'd actually be much the wiser anyway. Because he taught English. Austen, Hardy, Rowling and Horowitz. He felt safer talking about them than Alluren puplets and dwarf star alloys or even Stewart's missing sandwiches.

And, right now, he wasn't quite sure he was going to feel safe again. Not in an 'oh my God, the creatures from outer space are going to kill us tomorrow!' way, but in a 'nothing is ever going to be the same' way. Because once you've talked to an invisible alien puplet, how do you go back to discussing whether the narrative structure of *The Woman in White* helps or hiders the storytelling process or whether Gabriel Oak and Bathsheba –

'Mr Warner?'

It was Deena.

'Mr Warner, the Doctor asked if you're all right?'

Mr Warner looked at his pupil's face. So full of intelligence and inquisitiveness and concern and positivity and… innocence.

And he glanced at this mad, weird, bizarre and frankly terribly dressed Doctor person, who had paper that changed words, and devices to show you the invisible spectrum, and the ability to make Mrs Mulligan giggle, and he knew that what he had to do was very simple. Because it was the right thing to do.

'Yes, Doctor. Yes, I'm utterly fine. And okay, if we have an alien called Jess living on top of the scenery, then we have to make sure he's happy and well-fed and well-cared for over Christmas until his parents come to find him.' Mr Warner looked at Deena. 'Deena, you are in charge of sorting out a rota. Who apart from Colin and Stewart know about Jess?'

'Nobody else,' Colin piped up.

'Good, best to keep it that way. And heaven help me, you three, you'll never hear these words come from a teacher ever again, so mark this day in your diaries, MySpaces or whatever, but *do not tell your parents*.' Mr Warner then looked back at Deena. 'And no posting pictures on Facebook, all right? This is our secret. Between the five of us, okay?'

The Doctor bounded over and shook Mr Warner's hand. 'Oh you are good, Mr Warner. No, more than good, you're brilliant. *Molto bene* in fact.'

Mr Warner managed a smile, even though he'd just broken every rule in the book. 'Don't tell your parents', indeed – the headmaster would string him up for this!

'So, Deena,' Mr Warner continued, 'work out a rota. Twice a day, Jess needs feeding. Between the three of you, okay? And boys, this is a responsibility exercise. No "Sorry Mr Warner I needed to go into town to buy some trainers" – take responsibility for Jess. If that doesn't seem like the kind of thing you want to do over the holidays, fine, but you need to head home now.'

None of the kids moved.

'Fantastic,' Mr Warner said, cheered by the fact that he could rely on his students.

'And Doctor,' he said, turning to the strange young man. 'Doctor, can you write down for Deena everything you know that she needs to know about Jess?'

The Doctor nodded.

'Good. Now, we have one last thing to sort out.'

'What's that then?' asked the Doctor.

'Jess can't stay up there. Wherever he is, cos I can't actually see him.'

'Why not?' asked Colin, but Deena answered, slightly pompously 'Because tomorrow morning Mr Clarke is going to take the set down.'

Mr Warner nodded. 'Doctor, when you just spoke to Jess, did it... did he understand you?'

'No, it's like when you talk to a cat or a dog – they get your mood from the tone of your voice, your body language and all that, but the words mean nothing. It's just hoots and clicks to them. Jess is the same. But he knows we're not gonna hurt him.'

Mr Warner pondered this. 'Okay, but if he trusts you, that's a start.'

'Why?'

'Cos you, being the tallest and clearly the most adept at dealing with aliens, need to be the one to get him down from there and keep him happy and calm while we find him a tall perch that no one else can see, but is gettable to by the kids.'

The Doctor jumped off the stage, peered around the Assembly Hall, then looked out through a window. 'Trees?'

'Lots of them. What's to stop him going from one to another? We might lose him.'

The Doctor nodded. 'Good point. And I knew that, I was just testing. Deena? Thoughts as team leader?'

'The roof?'

Mr Warner nearly choked. 'And how do you lot get up there without breaking your necks? I'm all for looking after Jess, but not at any risk to you three.'

'Mr Warner's absolutely right,' the Doctor called from the window. 'Ahh... how often does the caretaker come in over Christmas?'

Mr Warner shrugged. 'No idea. He doesn't live on site, so maybe a couple of times a week.'

The Doctor headed towards the exit. 'Deena, Colin, Mr Warner, with me. Stewart, you okay staying with Jess?'

Stewart nodded.

'Talk to him,' Deena said.

'What about?'

'Read to him,' Mr Warner said, and climbed off the stage, crossing to where his bag was lying. He opened it and fished out a book.

He passed it up to Stewart. '*Alice Through the Looking Glass*. Brilliant book. Won't do you any harm to read it either to be honest, Stewart. Just read it to him while I find out what the Doctor's planning.'

He followed the Doctor down the school corridor, as the tall man stuck a head in various classrooms, the staff room (oh please, don't use the staff room!) and finally stopped at one of the smaller classrooms.

'Who uses this?'

Deena answered. 'Year 3.'

'Hence being small desks and chairs. And, therefore, the kids least likely to come to the school building during the holidays. Marvellous.'

And he bounded into the room and reached up. The ceiling was illuminated by a number of large plastic trays, each containing three fluorescent tubes.

He grabbed a chair and clambered onto it and then onto a desk, then reached up and quickly removed the tubed lights from one of the trays, passing them gently back to Colin and Deena.

Mr Warner realised he was going to put Jess in the plastic tray. 'Invisible to teachers and caretakers,' he said by way of explanation, 'and if Deena, Colin and young Stewart are the only ones who ever come in here, Jess should be safe.'

A COUPLE OF MINUTES LATER, THE DOCTOR RETURNED from the assembly hall, his arms held oddly, with Stewart trailing behind. He gently laid what Mr Warner could only guess was the soft, furred body of Jess in the tray. As he withdrew his hands, the tray moved as Jess settled and mewled, contentedly.

'Tell you what, Jess,' the Doctor said. 'I'll get Deena to show me where she found you and set up a sub etheric beam locator, attuned to Alluren frequencies. That way, your parents, who I bet are very anxious about you right now, will be able to lock onto it. Then I'll get a reading in my TARDIS when they're in range and arrange for them to collect you. But it's very important you stay put. Right here. The kids and lovely Mr Warner over there, they'll make sure you get food and water and, I reckon, more love and attention than you'll know what to do with. Lucky old Jess.'

'Is he safe up there, Doctor?' Mr Warner asked. 'If the Caretaker comes by and sees the lights aren't working, he'll try to repair them.'

The Doctor nodded and got out his pen device thing. He located the light switch on the wall and pointed the device at it. The end glowed blue and then he stepped back.

Mr Warner walked over and looked. The screw heads that held the light switch in place were smoothed off. No way to get a screwdriver in there now.

'Over Christmas, it'll take him ages to get a new facia for that, even if he notices something's wrong. Assuming Ma and Pa Alluren turn up before the end of the Christmas holidays, I can put that right and the caretaker will never realise.' He grinned. 'Trust me, I'm a Doctor.'

And Mr Warner did.

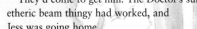

OVER THE NEXT FEW DAYS, MR WARNER MADE SURE HE was at the school whenever Deena's rota kicked in, just to let the kids in and out, and make sure nothing untoward happened.

And, if he was honest, in the hope that as time passed, the veil might be lifted from his eyes and he'd be able to see Jess as the kids did, instead of just hearing the mewls and seeing the lighting tray shift slightly as he ate and drank, or was put back in after one of the boys took him outside to do his business in the bracken behind the playing fields.

He was so proud of the way the kids handled all this. In years gone by,

some schools had brought in hamsters and rabbits to give kids who didn't have pets at home something to look after, to give them a sense of responsibility and something constructive to do over the school holidays.

This was slightly different. This was top secret and something shared only by Deena and her rotas, Colin and his pencils and questions, and Stewart and his sandwiches and ever present Tesco bag (which had turned up, complete with clothes, in the toilets where some other kid had unkindly hidden them. That was something Mr Warner would deal with in the new term.)

As the week passed, Mr Warner was positive he saw changes in the three kids – as if the responsibility was doing them good. Jess was a good influence. So, too, was the Doctor, probably. Although Mr Warner hadn't seen him, Deena said that one day she'd bumped into him in the Quiet Courtyard, examining the tree where she'd first found Jess.

Mr Warner was happy, too. He had something to do with his holiday, instead of trying to summon up the courage to ask Mrs English out.

One day, he promised himself. But he needed to see this little project through first. Priorities and all that.

ON THE EIGHTH DAY, MR WARNER ARRIVED AT THE SCHOOL, but the classroom was empty.

And the fluorescent lights were back on.

Mr Warner felt his heart race – had something gone wrong? Had the caretaker fixed the switch after all? Had something awful happened?

He checked the light switch – perfect, the screw heads defined once more. Everything back as it ought to be.

Then he heard a sound, a low rumble, a mewl.

'Jess…' he breathed, and realised it came from the Quiet Courtyard, where Deena said she had first found Jess all those days ago.

Trying not to run like a giddy schoolboy, a mix of anticipation and fear in his chest, Mr Warner made his way quickly down the corridor, through the double doors, and out into the patio area known as the Quiet Courtyard, so called because kids weren't allowed to scream and yell, and no mobiles or MP3 players were allowed. It was dotted with silver birch trees and wooden benches so kids could read and chill out.

The Doctor was there, head craned back as he looked up at something the height of the top of the silver birch.

Deena and Colin were there, too, but no sign of Stewart.

Of course, it wasn't his day on – Deena's rota was nothing if not fair.

And there was that mewling sound again. It wasn't Jess. It must, of course, be the parents.

They'd come to get him. The Doctor's sub etheric beam thingy had worked, and Jess was going home.

The Doctor was holding up his little wallet of paper again.

Deena was crying, Colin put a protective arm around her. She didn't shrug it off.

'They're taking him home, Mr Warner,' she said through the tears. Tears of sadness mixed with happiness. Jess' parents had found him.

'You did so well to look after him, Deena,' the Doctor said, without averting his gaze from the Alluren adults. 'You too, Colin. And they want you to thank Stewart as well.'

Colin nodded. 'Will we ever see Jess again?'

A mewl. Mr Warner smiled. That was Jess, he could hear the sad goodbye in its tone.

The Doctor shook his head. 'They've got a long way to go home, Colin. They were holidaying in this system when Jess got lost and ended up here. I don't think they're coming back any time soon.'

He grinned at the kids suddenly, a marvellous, positive, engaging grin that Mr Warner wished some of the teachers at school could give their pupils now and again.

'But you never know.'

Deena and Colin gasped suddenly and shielded their eyes.

'Typical teleports,' the Doctor said. 'Always with the brightness and fierceness. Spots in front of my eyes for hours now, I bet.'

'Goodbye Jess,' Deena murmured, as Colin led her away, and over to one of the benches.

'Stewart'll be sorry he missed that,' Mr Warner said quietly to the Doctor. 'Mum and Dad Alien, teleports, all that stuff.'

The Doctor gave Mr Warner a sideways look, almost pitying. Then grinned and called over to the kids.

'Colin!'

Colin looked up. 'Doctor?'

'You do art, don't you.'

Colin nodded.

'I want you to draw a picture, before term starts again. Little bit of homework. You don't mind, do you?'

Colin shrugged. 'Course not. What do you want?'

The Doctor whispered in Colin's ear. Mr Warner frowned as Colin looked at the Doctor, then him, then back to the Doctor. Then he and Deena stood up and left the courtyard.

'See you next week, Mr Warner,' Deena mumbled.

'See ya, kids,' Mr Warner called back. Then he stared at the Doctor. 'What did you ask Colin to draw?'

The Doctor held out a hand to Mr Warner, who responded automatically and the Doctor shook it. 'Wish I'd had teachers like you, Mr Warner. Might've turned out as well as the kids you're in charge of.'

'Are you off then?'

'Oh yes. Galaxies to see, systems to protect, people to meet. Goodbye Mr Warner. Keep that mind open, you never know what you might see.'

Mr Warner took a deep breath. 'You asked Colin to draw the Allurens, didn't you? For me.'

The Doctor smiled. 'A present for a good teacher.'

Mr Warner shrugged. 'The kids could see them, and that's far more important. And now I know there are aliens out there. Up there even.' He looked up to the sky, curiously bright and blue for a winter's morning. 'And that they're looked after by you.'

Mr Warner looked back to where the Doctor had stood, but he was gone. Mr Warner was alone in the Quiet Courtyard. Alone with his memories, his pride in his pupils, and a feeling of being part of something larger. Something... well, *universal*.

And he smiled.

'Right Mrs English,' he murmured to no one in particular. 'I wonder if you'd fancy a spot of dinner tonight...?'

THE END